Fate

Vs.

Destiny

By

Graysen Morgen

2012

Fate vs. Destiny © 2012 Graysen Morgen

Triplicity Publishing, LLC

ISBN-13: 978-1477410691

ISBN-10: 1477410694

Printed in the United States of America

First Edition – 2012

Cover Design: Triplicity Publishing, LLC

Interior Design: Triplicity Publishing, LLC

Also by Graysen Morgen

Falling Snow

Just Me

Love, Loss, Revenge

Natural Instinct

Secluded Heart

Submerged

Acknowledgements

Special thanks to Lee Fitzsimmons, the person who spends countless hours correcting my mistakes.

Dedication

To my loving partner, thank you for supporting my dreams and understanding my mistakes when I don't even understand them myself.

One

A long anticipated, late summer night's sleep ended with an ear-piercing screech of Waltz music and a vibration rattle as the cell phone on the nightstand lit up with an incoming call. The nude figure under the thin silk sheet rolled towards the ringing sound, one sun-tanned arm poked its hand out fumbling for the obnoxiously loud device.

"Greer!" A raspy, half-asleep voice spoke out.

"This is Walter Hudson with the NTSB-Aviation Department-Washington office. We have a major accident reported just outside of La Guardia in New York. Your flight leaves in forty-five minutes, the Crash Crew is en route. Your itinerary has been faxed to your office, Agent Greer."

Logan Greer rubbed her tired eyes, cursing silently into the night. *Why the hell did I choose this career?* Her lazy form rose from the bed as she stumbled into the bathroom. The cold water under the faucet was penetrating her skin like icicles as she splashed the sleep from her face.

"Forty-five minutes, man they're getting ridiculous with this shit. One day I'm going to miss one of these red-eye flights and then whose ass will be on the line? I can bet you it won't be mine. They've known for

1

over an hour and they wait until the last goddamn minute to call someone about it." Luckily, she kept a travel bag packed in the closet. She threw it on the floor as she pulled on a pair of jeans, a black polo shirt with the NTSB logo on the front left breast, and black Doc Marten shoes. As if out of routine, she tucked her black Sig-Sauer compact .45 into its waistband holster in the back of her pants, and she slid her investigator badge into one rear pocket, and cell phone into the other, all with precision movement.

Ten minutes after the night ending phone call, Logan was walking out of her condo building towards her black Ford Sport Trac. She glanced down at the thin silver band around her left wrist.

"Hmm…ten minutes and counting…oh, you're good Greer, damn good!"

She reached blindly into the passenger seat for the khaki colored ball cap. She slid it over her short dirty blonde hair and drove off into the darkness towards Jacksonville International Airport.

***

The First Class Flight Attendant stopped abruptly to help Logan store her bag into the overhead compartment.

"What about your briefcase? I think we have room for it up here." The tall brunette smiled at the slightly shorter woman standing next to her.

"No, uh…I need to…keep this out." Logan mumbled as she reached for the black case and ducked below the compartment to get to her window seat. She knew the seat next to her would be empty, the NTSB tried to keep the emergency flights as private as possible. There was no need to alert someone sitting on a perfectly good plane, about a devastating one that just crashed.

Logan took her laptop out and started inputting the accident data that the Washington Office faxed to her office. Luckily, this would be a short flight since it was non-stop. That rarely happened in the airline industry anymore. Just about every flight had a stop with some sort of lay over in the middle of nowhere. In the case of a lay over flight only that would leave her delayed, the NTSB would send their Crash Crew with her on a private Leer Jet. Usually, she was the first one to go and all alone since she was the Investigator In Charge or IIC, it was her job to be the National Transportation Safety Board representation and head up the entire accident investigation.

***

Logan was the first passenger off the plane since she was practically standing when it landed. One of the perks of getting in and out of the airport in a hurry was not checking any baggage. She walked right passed the long lines at baggage claim and towards the rental car area. *Suckers.*

"Can I help you, Ma'am?" The salt and pepper haired man at the counter called out to her. She pulled the badge out of her pocket, her Driver's License was tucked behind her NTSB Identification on one side of the leather fold and a shiny metal eagle encircled by *National Transportation Safety Board* was on the other. Logan handed both her license and badge fold to the man.

"Ah, yes, Miss Greer, we have an SUV saved for

you." He tapped the keys on the computer in front of him and handed her few pages of papers. "Sign here and initial here, here, and here. Then sign again down here."

Logan was happy to see the Black Explorer had a built in navigation system. "I don't have to fumble with a map in a city I've barely been in. How the hell did that happen?" She punched in the GPS coordinates that were on her fax and followed the voice prompts. The voice in the dash was highly upset when the driver took a wrong turn to enter the nearest Starbucks drive-through.

"Oh shut the hell up, I'm getting coffee. Excuse me if I made an invalid left turn."

The machine was back on track and Logan was drinking a Grande Mocha. Before she knew it, she was already at the roadblock. She pulled over to the police barricade and stuck her badge out of the window.

The young female officer gave her a wink as she pointed towards the escort truck parked a few feet away. "That truck is with you guys. He'll take you to the wreckage Ma'am." Logan nodded and drove off behind the other black SUV.

She could see the smoke rolling above the wooded trees about a hundred yards away. In the beginning, every accident felt as if it were the very first one, the tiny hairs on the back of her neck stood on end, goose bumps rose on her arms, and she quivered slightly. Her hands were cold and clammy. She brought the Explorer to a stop and looked through the open window at the smoldering fireball, barely three-hundred feet away.

She was immediately bombarded by NTSB and FAA field investigation members, followed by arrogant Police officers when she stepped out of the vehicle. She

4

merely shoved her badge fold in their faces as she took in the scenery. There were metal fragments scattered as far as she could see, black smoke filled the air from the still smoldering jet fuel, and the smell of burning flesh mixed gruesomely with it. She could barely hear the people talking to her over the loud generators and background chatter of fifty people talking at once. White 'official' tents decorated the outskirts of the main wreckage area. As Logan walked closer to the enormously large crater, she could see what would have once been the fuselage torn in two with jagged metal fragments sticking out on all sides, and wires protruding in every direction. As she kept walking, she could see what appeared to be a wing all twisted and mangled a few feet away. *Gotta get the worst part over Greer.* She winced only once as she continued examining the debris along the path to the main tent.

Inside she found the person she was looking for. A young, slightly shorter woman with an olive complexion and very light brown, honey blond colored hair pulled back in a bun walked slowly over to her. If Logan had to guess, the woman was younger than herself, probably still in her twenties.

"Can I help you?" The woman winked as she spoke softly.

"I'm the NTSB Investigator In Charge, Agent Logan Greer." She extended her right hand.

"I'm Brooke McCabe with the FAA, nice to meet you." She shook her hand and looked her up and down openly sizing up her competition. She was expecting a man when she heard the name of the IIC.

Oh, give it a rest you piss ant, you're stuck with me for as long as this thing takes so deal with it. Logan thought to herself.

"Well, I guess we should get started. I need to go meet with my field team. They should be here by now. That's my cell number if you can't reach me on the radio." Logan gave a slight nod as she handed the woman her business card.

***

Logan gathered up all of the NTSB members and went under one of the tents. The morning sun had barely risen and she already had small sweat droplets beading up on her forehead. *The first week of September is supposed to be cooler than a hundred degrees, at least in New York.* She glanced around at the twenty or so men and women staring patiently at her.

"I'm Agent Greer, Investigator In Charge. Anything and everything you find, hear, think, or see, goes through me first. I'm not here to make friends nor am I hear to baby sit. We all have a job to do. I trust all of you know exactly what that is." She only recognized some of the faces since the NTSB has agents all over the United States. They don't have to send the same ones to every crash site, except for the IIC which basically is called to head up the investigation at every major accident. The athletic looking, bluish-green eyed blond leaned back against the small folding table behind her and opened her palm pilot that she'd uploaded the data into. "This was a Boeing 727...flight number 897 New York to Dallas...pilot, co-pilot, and three crew members...110 passengers...115 casualties on scene. The ATC reports the pilot having a mechanical failure at 23:14 and was turning due north, heading back towards

La Guardia when flight 897 disappeared from the radar at 23:28. No one on the ground witnessed the plane coming down. There were however, reports of a loud boom at approximately 23:32. So far, this is all I have to go on. I need you and you." She pointed to a man and a woman to her left. "Both of you gather up any one who heard anything. We need official statements from everyone. It doesn't matter if they've already given them to the FAA."

She looked over to her right and informed three people standing there that they needed to drive back to town to the airport and get statements from everyone that had contact with that plane before it took off. "Take another person with you and go to the Air Traffic Control center and get statements from everyone in the control tower. As for the rest of you, we are here to recover all of the wreckage and try to piece this plane back together. Hopefully, we will find the Black Box before the end of the week. The Cockpit Voice Recorder and Flight Data Recorder should be able to lead us in some sort of direction. Does anyone have any questions?" She looked around as the group broke up.

When Logan finally checked into her hotel room, it was two a.m. She was lucky that one of her team members had fled to McDonalds late in the evening for the group. She fought off heartburn from the sloppy Big Mac and large fries that she inhaled. Just as she was about to doze off her cell phone rang loudly with the sound of a Waltz as it shook wildly on the table.

"Greer."

"Hello Agent Greer, this is Brooke McCabe. Did I wake you?"

"No, I'm sure you know I just got into my hotel. What can I do for you?" She was too tired to be annoyed at this point. She had spent the rest of her day avoiding the FAA Investigator at all costs.

"I was just making sure you knew we had a meeting at 05:00. I didn't get to talk to you before you left this evening."

"Yes, I'm aware of it. I'll be there."

***

The meeting had gone rather well for Logan she only had a small pissing contest with the FAA over the results of the CVR and FDR and who was credited for finding it. The Pilot had radioed the control tower stating that the tail rudder was not engaging. ATC instructed him to change course and head back to La Guardia.

Logan drank a cup of the only decent coffee she could find. She bent down and brushed some dirt off her pants. Brooke McCabe walked up behind her and unknowingly put her hand into the small of Logan's back. Both women jumped at the light touch. The shorter, petite woman backed away wondering what the hell she had just laid her hand on. Logan's light bluish green colored eyes grew very large and changed to dark blue as she turned towards the woman behind her.

"Can I help you?" Her voice was deeper than normal.

"Are you packing heat there, Agent Greer?" Brooke rolled the words off her tongue in a low sexy drawl.

"Yes, Miss McCabe, I have a concealed permit and I'm a government official. Do you have a problem with that?" Logan shot back at her with a raised eyebrow. *You'd be good for a roll in the sheets.* She thought when she felt the tension in her body relax slightly.

"No." She ran her hand gently down Logan's arm. "You look nice today."

"As opposed to yesterday?" Logan laughed slightly. "My first day on scene is usually hell. I didn't feel like wearing a pants suit and silk shirt yesterday, but today is a new day, and I'm suppose to be dressed like a government agent. Besides, I need to deal with the press as well as the Mayor. Obviously you are too since you're wearing a skirt." *Short enough for me to see just about everything you're purposely letting me see.*

Brooke ran her hand down her thigh past the point high up on her leg where the tight black skirt stopped. "Yes well we can't have our government employees slumming now can we, Agent Greer?" Logan's cell phone rattled on her belt as the Waltz music played.

"Please excuse me." She stepped away.

"Greer."

"Hello Gary, did you get all of the statements?"

"Yes, Ma'am." A male voice answered back.

"Great, meet me in the conference room at my hotel."

***

Four long grueling weeks later, all of the documentation that was gathered confirmed Logan's hypothesis. The planes tail rudder was not functioning properly when the plane took off, the mishap caused the plane to veer off course, and as the pilots tried to recover they lost control of the vertical direction of the plane. They plunged twenty thousand feet to the ground at a forty-five degree angle, straight into a wooded area.

Logan sat in her hotel room typing up the first part of her accident report. "Well, in the morning I'll be back in Florida and I can finish this at my desk, no need to bother with it tonight." She took her gun and holster off her belt and slid it into her briefcase on the table. Her mind drifted briefly to the dramatic incident that caused her to begin caring a firearm. Logan stretched her frame, feeling the tense pressure in her muscles from not working out during the last four weeks, crawling in and out of a smashed up heap of metal, and helping to move bits and pieces around the hanger where the wreckage remained. She glanced down at her left wrist. *I bet the bar's still open downstairs.*

As soon as she stepped out of the elevator, she saw Brooke McCabe, her long honey colored hair hung down to the small of her back. She was still wearing her black skirt suit. Logan couldn't hide the lust in her eyes.

"Well, what do I owe the pleasure, Agent Greer?"

"I was...uh...I wanted a drink. How are you Miss McCabe?"

"Please, call me Brooke, and do join me for drink."

Both women sat at a small table in the corner. Logan ordered a chilled glass of Navan, an expensive vanilla flavored Cognac and the woman across from her ordered Vodka with a splash of Cranberry. Logan was surprised when she saw Brooke's birth date on her Badge ID and noticed she was actually a couple years older than Logan. She decided to keep it to herself.

"Well, here's to the end of a long four weeks." Brooke stated with a wink. This was the first time Logan noticed that Brooke's eyes were almost the same viridian green color as her own, except Logan's seemed to change from green to blue depending on her mood. She also noticed how naturally beautiful the petite woman was.

"Yeah but, here's to the next month of paperwork on my desk because of it." Both women laughed as their glasses clinked together. Logan could feel the heat radiating off the woman in front of her. *My god she has to know what looking at me like that is doing to the fire between my legs, I'm only human.* Brooke slid her stocking covered foot inside the right leg opening of Logan's pants. The brief contact caused Logan's body to shutter and she splashed her drink on her shirt.

"Damn it!"

"We'd better get you upstairs, Agent Greer. You wouldn't want that drink to stain that pretty silk shirt you're wearing."

Brooke tossed a twenty on the table while Logan wiped the rest of the drink off her chin.

***

When the elevator doors shut, Brooke slammed Logan against the back wall with one hand in her short blonde hair and the other pinching a nipple under the sheer material. "Ah...god. You're gonna...make me...come right here...if you..."

Brooke claimed Logan's mouth with her own fiercely searching with her tongue when Logan's lips parted to allow the entrance. Logan ran her hands down Brooke's hips and hiked the skirt up on both sides. She gripped tight butt cheeks and thrust Brooke up against her thigh. The elevator chimed since it was about to stop on Brooke's floor. Their interlude came to a screeching halt when the doors pulled apart.

"My room's this way." Brooke grabbed Logan's hand and intertwined their fingers, pulling her unsteadily off the wall.

The door to her room was barely shut before she was fumbling with the buttons on Logan's blouse. Logan had Brooke's skirt up around her waist exposing the black lace thong underneath when she ripped the sheer panty hose off her. Brooke bent slightly forward and ran her lips down the uncovered cleavage at the opening of Logan's bra.

"I'm gonna make you come so hard." Brooke's voice was thick with lust when she spoke.

She loosened Logan's belt and dropped her pants to the floor. She began massaging the soft wet folds between Logan's thighs through her panties. Logan unbuttoned Brooke's top and tossed it to the floor. She unzipped the tight black skirt and backed away just enough to let it pass between them. She ran her hands down Brookes back, through her long hair, and pulled the woman tightly against her as she pressed her lips to Brooke's mouth. The kiss was long and mischievous, daring the other woman to take it further. As if on cue, Brooke pushed Logan back towards the bed. Both women lay down together, skin to skin. Brooke slid in between Logan's legs, spreading her thighs allowing herself to glide back and forth across her wet center. Logan choked back a loud moan when Brooke clenched a nipple between her lips and flicked it with her tongue.

"Oh...that feels so good!"

Logan ran her fingers along Brooke's swollen clit, slowly at first, teasing the woman above her. Brooke rocked back and forth sliding her wetness over Logan's hand until she entered her gently thrusting in and out.

"I'm gonna…oh god I'm coming…oh yeah, oh god!" Brooke threw her head back and slid her hand down to the wet throbbing muscles between Logan's thighs. Logan jumped with the contact and pushed her hips up into the hand that was touching her.

"That's it…let it go honey…"

"You're making me…ah!" Logan gripped the sheets as she released the lust that had been building up inside of her for the past four weeks.

***

At five a.m. Logan snuck out of Brooke's room with cat-like moves and made her way back to her own room. Her body was tender and sore in places that reminded her of the hours she just spent having sex. At eight-thirty she was on a plane leaning back with her eyes closed, finally headed home. *My god Greer, you're thirty years old, it's time to get your life together. A one night stand with the FAA Investigator is not the right direction!*

Brooke awoke to a note on the nightstand.

Thank you for a wonderful night. Maybe I'll see you again. Signed, Logan Greer.

"Well, Agent Greer, I'm sure I will definitely see you again."

Two

After being home just over a week, Logan finally made it down to the gym. Donning only a black sports bra and tiny black gym shorts, she sat on the floor and stretched her hands to touch the sneakers on her feet. The tight muscles expanded and contracted under soft tanned skin with every movement. Satisfied with her flexibility, she strapped the black gloves on her hands and walked over to the speed bag hanging from the stand in the corner next to the heavy bag. She started slowly with a rhythm of light punches. She kept up with the bag as it gained speed. Faster and faster, she threw her punches one after the other into the small bag. Arms burning, muscles loose, she turned to the heavy bag and began punching it. Harder and faster with sweat pouring from her face and glistening on her taut stomach. *One night stand with a total stranger*...jab...left...right left, left...right...*What the hell Greer, gotta hand it to you babe*...uppercut...right, right, left...left...quick right...*she was definitely hot, nothing like your usual type, but worth it*...She continued punching until her fists throbbed with pain. She could feel her knuckles bleeding inside the gloves she was wearing.

***

Two months had gone by since the major crash in New York was wrapped up. She was dealing with minor accidents day in and day out at Jacksonville International Airport, which was her home office. One of which totally took the icing on the cake and had her in knee high paperwork for a week and a half when a 757 bumped its nose into the terminal, shattering the glass and sending the waiting passengers scattering for safety. The waiting patrons suffered only minor injuries, cuts, and bruises, but the building structure on that wing of the airport had shut down for a month of repairs. She was sure that pilot would never be licensed to fly a paper airplane again, much less a million dollar plane. Logan sat at her desk typing the last of the notes on the airport safety inspections.

"When are you leaving, Agent Greer?" A young black man stood in her office doorway wearing an airport security uniform.

"Next week, I'll be in D.C. for about two weeks of meetings and then I leave for six weeks of airport safety inspections. Boy oh boy, I look forward to this time twice a year." He could sense the frustration in Logan's voice.

"I don't blame you. I'm not one for snow as high as a moose's ass either." Both of them laughed. Logan didn't know why, but for some reason she always enjoyed talking to him. He wasn't much younger than her she presumed.

"Well, I guess I better head home for the night. Try to stay out of trouble." She called back over her shoulder..."Hey Ricky, how about one night with no accidents, mistakes, wing benders, mishaps, or anything

15

else you guys like to call it." She grinned when he laughed at her.

***

Logan parked the Sport Trac in the spot marked eight-seventeen, the same number that matched her door. The eighth floor was the highest of the Condo tower and she occupied the space in one of the four penthouses. Hers was beachfront with a master room including a full his/her bath with a garden tub, a study, and a spare room with a separate bath. The kitchen had a small island and a bar with marbled tops that matched the marbled tile floor. The counter and island looked out over the living room area. The Study also looked out at the living area through French doors. The balcony had French doors leading from the master bedroom, as well as the kitchen, and then going around the corner over by the study. A large flat plasma TV hung on the wall in the corner and a large square marble-topped table sat on the floor in front of the L-shaped couch. The place was large enough for a family but cozy enough for one or two and was always in show condition since the owner was rarely home. Logan walked in and sat her keys on the small table in the foyer. Her briefcase went in the study on her desk and her gun and its holster went on the nightstand by her bed along with her badge fold.

Logan shed her business suit in exchange for loose fitting jeans, a black sweater over her white t-shirt, and Doc Marten's. She grabbed the other set of keys on the table, stuck her badge fold in her back pocket with her cell phone, and locked the door behind her. She waved to the front desk staff as she exited the elevator. On the left side of the building, there was a small section of storage units for the Condo owners. Logan walked over to number eight-seventeen. She made sure everything was numbered the same for her convenience when she bought her unit. As the door rose up she saw her pride and joy sitting there longing to come out and play, lusting to be rode hard and put up wet.

"Hey, Cat's Ass. Sorry I've been too busy for you. Momma wants to go for a ride!" She stood back and stared at the only love in her life...a Buell Lightning XB9 Sport bike, solid black, custom chrome exhaust, chrome wheels, and neon green lights underneath. She grabbed her black night riding glasses with light purple tinted lenses off the seat. She put her khaki ball cap on backwards, swung her leg over the seat, kicked it into neutral, and rolled the bike out of the garage. With a flick of the wrist, the machine roared to life, the exhaust thundered in her chest steadily with the beat of her heart and the vibration became one within her thighs. *God I've missed this.* She left the bike to idle as she closed the storage unit door. When she turned back towards the back of the bike, a smile curled on her lips. The tag read: CATSAZZ. A minute later, she was riding with the wind down the streets of Jacksonville Beach. *Free as a bird.*

She maneuvered the bike with perfect precision through the streets across the bridge to the local lesbian bar, Jane's Place. Not really in the mood to peruse the usual crowd for a one night stand, she parked the bike on the sidewalk and tucked the hat under the bungee cord storage net on the seat. A few women were outside smoking, some of whom she knew from coming to the bar. When she passed through the doors, Logan heard a few girls saying hey to her. She smile thinly and nodded.

As soon as she planted her butt on a stool, the bartender slid an ice-cold bottle of Foster's Lager down to her.

"Hey Logan, how the hell are ya girl?" The tall curly haired bartender smiled brightly at the woman in front of her.

"Not bad Bridgette. You?" Logan took a nice long swallow of the cold liquid. She could feel it tingle all the way to the bone. *God I haven't been out in so long.*

"Steady, the bar has its nights. I haven't seen you in months. What's up?"

"Yeah, I've been working a lot lately. In fact, I'm leaving Monday for two weeks, then, I come home for a week and leave for six more weeks after that." Logan nonchalantly ran a hand through her hair.

"Damn, I thought I had it rough… Did you ride? I thought I heard the bike."

"You know it. I figured I had better take it now before it gets too cold. I'll look like a damn Eskimo."

"Haha that I would like to see!"

"Me too!" An auburn haired woman sitting on the bar stool next to Logan spoke out. "Hi, I'm Carie." She extended her hand to Logan.

"Logan. Nice to meet you."

"That's a nice bike, I saw you come up."

"Thanks."

"You come here often?" The woman slid closer than Logan would've liked her to but she continued the conversation.

An hour later Carie nodded towards the door and Logan turned around to see an adorable young girl walk through the opening, laughing and talking to her friends. She was slightly shorter than Logan, but with the same athletic build and long naturally curly blond hair twisted

18

back and pulled up behind her head. She was wearing loose fit jeans, a small white t-shirt and flip-flops.

"She's fucking hot! I need to come here more often." The woman next to Logan spat out.

"She's more than that. She's..." Logan was thinking out loud and she knew she'd better stop. *She looks like a surf angel. Very similar to the one from my...oh my god the girl that comes to me in my dreams.* Logan shook her head at the faint touch of déjà vu. She hadn't been visited in her dreams lately by the mysterious blonde that seemed to haunt her.

Their conversation continued until the blond girl came up to the side of the bar across from Logan. Logan winked at her as the bartender walked out and hugged the stranger. They were obvious friends and the girl was more than likely a regular, and since Logan had been out of the loop for a while, she had no idea who this girl was.

Another beer later, karaoke was well underway and various lesbians were belching out songs for their lovers.

"So Logan, do you dance? Or sing?"

Logan was glad the lighting was too low for Carie to see her blush.

"No, I can dance and I think I can carry a tune, but I usually don't dance unless I'm drunk and I damn sure don't karaoke no matter how much I've drank. Since I'm on the bike tonight, we won't be seeing any of that."

Both women laughed.

"I can't believe it's midnight already. Time flies when you're having fun." Logan smiled thinking to herself. Carie had reached her limit long ago and continued to hold the light-headed buzz of alcohol in solitude. The cute little blond that she ogled in the doorway walked up next to Logan and she turned towards her. *She's even more adorable up close, my god she's young looking, has to be barely twenty-one.*

"You're...uh...shy aren't you?" Logan's mouth curled and her eyes glazed over as she fought to say something to the girl. *Oh, that's real smooth Greer.*

She simply shrugged her shoulders. "No. Not always." Her voice was sweet, but hoarse for such a small person, almost as if she had been yelling all day. The strange girl walked back over to her friends.

"She's definitely into you. God she's such a hottie," Carie whispered.

"Yeah, she's cute, but I don't think she's into me." Just as Logan finished her sentence the blond she was referring to walked up behind her and tugged her off of her stool, interlocked her fingers with Logan's, and pulled her to the dance floor. They threaded their bodies together instantly, a fit so perfectly matched it looked as though they were lovers. *Sittin' on the Dock of the Bay* played softly as Logan swayed slowly with this enticingly beautiful young woman in her arms.

She had the most naturally sweet smell. Logan could feel not only her body, but also her heart warming to the softness of this stranger. She was scared to hold on too tight, scared she might break the tender body in her arms, and damn scared of the intensity she was feeling deep inside her chest. All too quickly, the song was over and the other woman went back to her friends. Logan was burning with flames over every inch of her body that was warmed by this strangers touch. She gradually made her way back to the bar.

"Wow. That was weird." Carie, Logan's new bar friend sat there bug eyed.

"No shit. Talk about fire and ice."

"Hold that thought, here she comes." The unpredictable stranger walked back over to Logan who was standing with her back against the bar. They were face to face and Logan could see the light bluish gray eyes looking not just up at her, but directly into her soul. Slowly, the woman stepped forward. Logan mimicked her until their breasts and thighs were touching, hands, down by their sides, staring into each other's eyes. Logan was a few inches taller. They stood for mere seconds that felt as long as minutes. Finally, almost in sync, they thread their arms around each other as their lips met softly.

Logan leaned back, unsure how far to go with this mysterious woman in her arms. It felt like an all too familiar dream. The kiss didn't end as their lips parted to allow the introduction of their tongues to this soft cry of passion between them. Two total strangers glowing with desire for one another. To the naked eye, they looked like young lovers. The shorter blond backed away slowly. Logan bent down to her ear.

"What are you doing to me?" She whispered softly.

"Nothing, what are you doing to me?" The soft voice spoke back to her before she stepped away. Logan turned towards the bar and downed the last of her beer. She could feel the heat boiling under her skin. She turned back to see the strange young woman looking her way.

"What the fuck is with her?" Carie asked. She couldn't believe these two women had never seen each other before.

"I don't know. I've never had anything like this happen to me. I don't even know her damn name." Logan spoke to Carie shrugging her shoulders as the woman came back up to her.

"You gonna take me home?" The raspy soft, sweet voice asked casually.

"Uh…uh sure. Where do you live?" Logan had a whirlwind of scenarios rolling through her head.

"Up on Southside. You?"

"I live at the beach." The girl leaned against Logan's body and pressed her lips gently to Logan's, nibbling on her bottom lip. The kiss started slowly and progressed as Logan possessively put her hands in the small of the girl's back and pulled her tightly against her. When the kiss ended, the girl backed away again.

"I should probably ride with a friend. I don't need to take someone home from the bar." She looked quietly into Logan's eyes.

"Trust me. I can drive you home without sleeping with you. I'm not some horny guy."

"I know…look, I should go." She turned to walk away, Carie yelled out to her.

"Hey, what's your name?"

"Jensen," she said as the door shut behind her.

"I guess I should be going too. It was uh…nice meeting you Carie." Logan extended a hand to the woman next to her.

"Yeah you too, better luck next time."

"Yeah," Logan rolled her eyes. She hadn't intended on hooking up with anyone, or whatever you would call their sexual innuendo.

Logan walked out of the bar and noticed the girl…*Jensen*…standing there. She rubbed the small of her back as she walked by her. Jensen turned and pulled Logan into her arms and they embraced tightly, feeling the warmth once against from head to toe. Electricity flowed freely from one body to the next. Their lips touched in an inviting kiss that neither woman was ready to release. Their tongues dueled for entry between each others lips. Everything ended all too soon as Jensen pulled away once more.

"Goodnight," Logan muttered, slightly biting her bottom lip.

"Goodnight." Jensen winked at her.

***

Logan slid her hat on backwards and roared the bike to life once again. The neon glowing on the chrome looked like a green blob as she drove off into the night. All thoughts, rational or fallacious escaped her mind during the short journey home. All she wanted to do was ride that bike as fast as it would let her in an attempt to clear the cobwebs from her head. Instead, she obeyed the laws and drove home. Back in front of her Condo tower, Logan whipped the bike into the small storage bay and locked the door. She ran a trembling hand through her hair. Wide awake, unable to comprehend the events of the past few hours, her body raw, starving for the lost contact of the tiny hot body that had been in her arms most of the night. Logan walked towards the iron gate leading to the ocean, pausing briefly to enter her key code. The familiar salty breeze partially revived her senses, her nerves were terribly confused and vulnerable, she didn't walk far fearing she may melt right there in the sand.

"This is absurd Greer, get your act together." Both hands rubbed delicately along her face. *You didn't sleep with her; you'll probably never see her again.* "I know it was you, in my dreams I can't see your face, but I can feel your body. The way you touch me, you haunt me night after night. Why do you show yourself to me now? Why tonight? Damn it, go back to my dreams, you can't break my heart there!" *I'd blame it on the beer, but I only drank two, alcohol definitely had nothing to do with it.*

***

"Good Morning, Agent Greer. I can assume you're in the air?"

"Hello, Mr. Hudson. Yes, I should be touching down at Dulles in about twenty minutes." She squeezed the airplane phone that she held in her hand.

"Great, our meetings start in about two hours. I'll see you then."

She growled back to the dial tone. "Nice, I don't need to rent a car or put my bags in a hotel room. No way, I'll just fly right up to the god damn doors. Mind if I park the plane on the front lawn?"

The plane landed with a thud and skidded to a halt.

"I swear the FAA gives a license to just about any damn body these days. Even after 9/11 you'd think they would at least have some sort of qualifications to drive one of these things. My hard earned tax dollars pay for those guys to sit on their asses and not give two shits." The guy sitting across the aisle from Logan spat out as he unbuckled his seat belt. His wife tried to shush him but the entire first class section pretty much heard him voice his opinion. Logan couldn't help butting in.

"Sir, believe me, with the government using 'your

24

tax dollars' the way it does these days, you'd never know if one of their agents was on the same plane as you, hell he could be sitting right next to you. If he believes the plane is safe enough for his ass," She looked over at his wife. "Then I'm sure it's safe enough for you." *Jackass!* Logan grabbed her briefcase and marched in line one by one down the terminal.

***

After four hours of note taking, coffee drinking, sleepy eyed, mono-toned meetings, Logan made her way to the ground floor of the twenty-story building. When she exited the building, she retrieved the voicemail that was left on her cell phone sometime during the morning madness.

"I heard you were in town…I'd like to see you again. Call me." Logan couldn't hide the flush of red heat in her checks or the slight curl in her lips when she recognized the sexy, sultry voice.

"Greer, you're a magnet for complication." *Yeah, I'll call you McCabe; call you when I'm in dire need of water to put out the flames between my legs.* Logan shook her head and walked towards her rented SUV.

***

Three weeks into her Airport Safety Inspections, Logan was standing with the Chief Safety Inspector of LAX in Los Angeles, when her cell phone rang its usual vibrating ridiculous Waltz tone that she hated, but was too lazy to change.

"Greer."

"Agent Greer, this is Walter Hudson with the NTSB-Aviation Department."

"Yes, what can I do for you?" Logan was not use to getting calls from someone in the Washington Office, except her boss, unless it was urgent or an accident. Most of the time they called her local regional office and she got back to them if she was out in the field.

"Where are you?" The dominant male voice questioned. Logan was confused, her eyebrows furled together.

"I'm at LAX, inspecting. Why?"

"We had a report of a runway accident there."

"When? I've been here for over an hour. I didn't hear anything and no one's called me except for you."

"I'm not sure, check it out, and get back to me. I don't have all of the details. The call came in from the FAA about twenty minutes ago."

Logan closed her phone and looked quizzically at the salt and pepper haired man next to her who was supposed to be in charge of the airport safety.

"Mr. Fuller, that was my Washington Office, they have a reported accident here."

"What? I would've..." He was cutoff in mid sentence when they heard a page over the airport intercom for him. He quickly dialed the number from the page. Two words into the call he grabbed Logan's wrist and snatched her with him. Both of them were running down the terminal towards the nearest outside employee exit. Logan figured the call she received was probably correct and no one bothered to alert the man in charge, the man whom happened to be next to her receiving his NTSB inspection. *I'll have someone's ass for this.* Logan thought to herself as she followed the running man. The inspector stopped a woman with a luggage truck coming their way.

"I need this...move...NOW!" He shoved the woman out of the other side as Logan climbed up on the small tractor. They took off at full speed.

"Does this thing go any faster?" Logan muttered.

"I have it floor boarded!" He shouted. As they rounded the turn towards the Air Traffic Control Tower, they could see the lights from the fire engines and a small cloud of smoke in the far off distance.

"I can't believe no one bothered to contact me! Damn it!" He spouted.

They pulled up next to one of the yellow fire trucks. Logan pulled her badge fold and shoved it in anyone's face that came near her. She noticed the large group of people in the background, some standing and hugging, others sitting staring patiently at the plane they had just stepped out of.

"I'm Agent Greer with the NTSB. I need to know what's going on here." A few of the airport employees turned towards her and then looked at the older man next to her. "NOW DAMN IT!" She annunciated as her voice raised high enough to grab the attention of the rescue crew. A guy in a gray and blue grounds crew uniform ran over to her.

"Ma'am, I saw the whole thing."

"Talk!"

"Uh...I...well this plane...it just left uh...gate...gate D19. It started out...I saw it on runway...um...A2." The man was shaking and could barely speak a full sentence.

"Okay?" Logan was patient, thinking back to the first crash site she'd ever seen. *Mangled metal fragments and the smell of burnt flesh, voices screaming in the distance singed her brain.*

"They were off…off the ground and then…I don't know…the plane…it just fell from the sky…nose first. Like…this." He gestured a movement with his hand.

"Fuller," Logan shouted over to the inspector, who was now working with his crew. "I need written statements from everyone that got off of that plane, everyone that saw the accident, and everyone that was anywhere near that plane before it left the gate. Try gate D19, this crewman said it left from there."

"Yes, Ma'am."

Logan turned back towards the rescue workers that were still pulling bodies from the wreckage.

"Only pull out the ones that are close to the fire, and of course everyone that is alive. Leave everything else for the photographs." She grabbed two Policemen that were standing nearby. "You and your friend here go rope off a radius of one hundred yards around this wreck. No one comes within a hundred yards of that mark unless you speak directly to me. I mean that gentlemen. NO ONE! This is an official investigation and everyone here is at high risk."

***

The small DC9 was, crushed from the nose back to the wings. Anyone that had been sitting in the front section of the plane was considered a casualty. Most of the passengers in the rear of the plane escaped with minor injuries and the few that were in between had been air lifted and ground transported to the local hospital with serious injuries. She tossed her suit jacket on one of the fire trucks, pulled her shirt loose so that the gun against her back was covered, and rushed to help the rescue guys in the middle of the wreckage. She helped pry back the insulated steel. Wires were hanging down, sparking everywhere. Heavy black smoke filled the air, burning her lungs. The fire was quickly contained. All that was left was the recovery of the pilot and co-pilot bodies. Logan winced at the smell and closed her eyes when she passed the broken up charred bodies down the line of workers. She cautiously stepped away from the fuselage and moved towards the tail of the plane where officials were working to remove the black box containing the CVR and FDR.

"I'll need to hear that as soon as we are ready for transmission." Dusk was setting in, the bright flood lights lit up the white debris field scattered around the tainted plane.

"I'm sure you were going to wait for me, Agent Greer." Logan turned towards the familiar voice.

"Hello, Miss McCabe." The beautiful woman with honey colored hair, an olive complexion, and piercing green eyes was standing a foot away. "Of course I was waiting for the FAA. Just as you guys wait for me, which by the way *is* protocol," Logan stated. Brooke winked, the edge of her lips curled into a seductive smile. Logan felt the blood rush to places she hadn't felt in weeks. Without warning, she knew she was wet and aching for her fire to be extinguished.

"Are you okay, your shirt's torn, you look like you were on the plane." Brooke noticed the soot, mixed with blood and dirt from the plane on Logan's clothes and in her hair. She looked like she'd been through hell and back.

29

"I assisted with the recovery." Logan spoke softly, trying not to bring up everything she had witnessed in the past few hours.

"You better go get a Tetanus shot or something ."

"No offense Miss McCabe, but I'm the NTSB Investigator In Charge, I do believe I know the regulations. Besides, I just had one about three months ago when I was working another investigation and cut myself."

Once inside the small office full of equipment in the airport, both women and a few other officials including Fuller listened carefully to the CVR. All of the data matched the statements from the ATC. Logan stood up from the table, one hand running vigorously through her hair, the other planted firmly on the desktop.

"I just don't understand how a god damn plane can crash at one of our nations largest airports and no one bothers to contact the CSI. On top of that, a half hour goes by before the airport main staff is alerted that there is even an incident. I was on the goddamn grounds and had to hear about this through my Washington Office on my cell phone. The...no offense..." She looked over towards Brooke. "FAA was alerted from the control tower, they were the ones that informed the NTSB, not the ATC. I want to know how this happened. Someone is responsible for dropping the ball. The only people on the scene of that accident were rescue officials and grounds crewmen. The Chief Safety Inspector and I were the last to arrive after the fire was detained. There is no excuse why the ATC didn't contact him or me knowing I was on the grounds today for an inspection."

She walked around the small table with all eyes directed towards her. "On top of that, none of the flights were shut down. Everyone knows after 9/11 any and all incidents cause the remaining incoming and outgoing flights to shut down until the situation is resolved, especially if it happens at any airport facility. Someone's ass is on the line here. You can bet I will put a full investigation on this whole facility. This is by far the largest breach in safety control that I have ever seen. The NTSB will have no choice but to seek action against all parties involved during the events before and after this accident." Logan stretched her neck and shook her head. She turned towards the door and exited the room. *God damn idiots! This airport is run by god damn idiots!* Halfway down the hall, she took her cell phone out of her pocket and speed dialed number four.

"NTSB Accident Office, this is Walter Hudson."

"This is, Agent Logan Greer…"

"Greer, what's the story? Last I heard there was a crash report but no one confirmed anything from the location." He sat back in his desk chair rubbing his forehead, not realizing the late hour in his time zone.

"Sir, there was a safety violation, somehow, somewhere, someone forgot to notify the CSI of the accident. The ATC however did remember to call the FAA, as I'm sure you already know."

"What the hell, you mean nobody called the Airport's own safety inspector?"

"Yes, sir. I was with him most of the afternoon, and when my call came in from you, we had no idea that there was anything going on. Nothing was shut down."

"Damn it, this is serious Greer. Do you need me to send anyone out there to assist you?"

"No…" She rubbed her eyes with her right hand. "I'm fine. This just may take a while. My inspections will be postponed until I wrap up here, probably in a few weeks."

"Keep me updated on everything you find out. Get with the CSI and set up a secure fax line and data port so we can have direct communication. Did your investigation team arrive at a decent time?"

"Yes sir, they were here about two hours after I was on the scene. I'll make sure we set up that COM line before I leave the facility tonight."

"Greer, watch out for the corrupt and disgruntled employees and passengers."

"Yes Sir, you don't have to remind me." *I have my own reminders.*

* * *

Three weeks later, Logan found herself amidst a mountain of paperwork. Faxes and emails were coming in faster than she could read them. Her cell phone seemed to never stop ringing. All of the plane wreckage was moved into an empty hanger on the eastside of the terminal building. She spent numerous hours crawling through that twisted pile of foul smelling metal, and weighing the facts versus the statements, nothing seemed to match up. The mechanic's logs were all up to date, yet no one could give her specifics on noted and highlighted areas. The same thing was happening with the ATC log books. Everyone knew the emergency steps, yet no one knew why they were not followed. One thing was for sure, there was not one person in that airport pointing a finger. Logan threw her hands up and walked out of the paper-filed room, Brooke McCabe was strolling down the hallway in her direction. *Shit.*

"Agent Greer, it's nice to see you again. I've been trying to reach you. We need to put our heads together on this situation."

Logan stretched her neck and felt the binding tension in her muscles. "I know we need to discuss a few areas, I've been extremely busy with NTSB documents. You're probably pretty much done here. I know you'll be leaving soon..."

"Yes, as a matter of fact I'm leaving tomorrow so I was hoping to get this taken care of tonight. If that's possible..."

"Join me for a cup of coffee. Fuller's been bringing me Starbucks from somewhere in here, damn if I know where it is though."

Both women walked around the large airport until they found the food court. Logan ordered a Grande Mint Mocha and Brooke settled for a Carmel Latte'. When the two reappeared in front of the small office, Mr. Fuller was just about to head home for the night.

"I hate to leave you, Agent Greer, but I'm afraid my eyes won't cooperate with me any longer." He smiled briefly. Logan nodded back to him.

"I'm use to it, I'll be fine here, Fuller. Have a good night."

When the older gentleman left the room, Brooke turned towards the woman next to her slightly brushing her hand over Logan's thigh. Logan's muscle twitched with the light touch.

"I do believe we have some notes to compare, Agent."

I'm sure you want to compare more than notes McCabe. You can't hide the seduction in your eyes. Who knows, I may just let you, at this point it's a win-win situation.

Logan took her suit jacket off completely aware of the gun touching her backside. She sat in the reclining desk chair, her lap top glowing brightly in front of her. Brooke was leaning against the desk on the opposite side of the tiny room. Logan peered over the top of her screen...*You know exactly what you're doing to me...the serious 'fuck me' eyes are distracting as hell.*

"Here, I have the head grounds crewman's statement. You should see this." Brooke walked up behind Logan and leaned down next to Logan's ear to peer over her shoulder at the screen. Hot breath effortlessly flowed across her neck making Logan's muscles tightened and contract. As the beautiful goddess-looking woman leaned closer to point out a detail of the statement, her breast grazed Logan's back. She could feel Brooke's rigid nipples against her. Logan tilted her head back until she could feel Brooke's wet lips on her neck. Logan turned to capture Brooke's mouth in a slow grueling kiss that rapidly turned seductive when she ran her tongue around her lips, teasingly slow and sucked her bottom lip. Logan's body was on fire, burning with lust deep inside. She grabbed Brooke's waist, tugging her around the front of the chair and into her lap. Brooke sat with her skirt pulled up, straddling Logan's lap, rocking her hips against Logan's. Logan slid Brooke's blouse open releasing her breasts from the black lace bra and seizing a hard nipple between her lips with one swift motion, flicking her tongue across the rigorous surface.

"Ah...that feels so good." Brooke tossed her head back thrusting her breasts towards Logan's burning mouth. Logan removed her gun and set it inside her open briefcase next to the desk, then stood up with the smaller woman still wrapped around her, she stepped forward sitting Brooke on the desk, thrusting her hips against Brooke's. Brooke frantically removed the buttons from Logan's dress shirt stripping it from her shoulders. She unclasped the satin bra, exposing firm round breasts. Brooke absorbed one nipple with her mouth and massaged the other with her hand. Logan worked Brooke's panties down her legs and stroked the slick wet folds between her thighs. Brooke urged her hips forward and wrapped her legs around Logan's waist, as she ran her hands down Logan's tight smooth skin and into the waistline of her pants. With one skilful move, her hand was swimming in a sea of hot liquid between Logan's legs. Both women were climbing the walls of desire, begging for release as they rubbed and squeezed each others engorged clit at the same time.

"Oh yeah...ah..." Her bottom lip between clinched teeth, Logan howled with pleasure. Brooke could barely breathe, completely engulfed with flames from Logan's touch.

"God Logan...oh you feel so good...yes...uh..." She grabbed a head-full of Logan's blonde hair with her free hand while the other stroked faster and harder. Logan bent her head forward meeting Brooke's aching mouth with her own. They simultaneously freed each other at will. All the tension dissipated from Logan's body as she felt the last wave of orgasm shutter through her body. Both women flustered from the realization of the rampage carnality that passed between them.

***

Logan drove around downtown L.A., not sure

35

what she was looking for, hoping it would come to her when she found it. Her eyes lit up when she passed a hole in the wall bar, 'Main St. Blues'. *Hmm...*She turned the SUV around and parallel parked it on the street. The tiny place was just as small as it appeared to be. A horse shoe shaped bar stood out from the wall. A mysterious young woman sat behind an extremely large piano directly across the room versifying a heart wrenching, semi-sweet blues melody. Her drummer sat to her left and her guitar player on the right. To the naked eye and untrained ear, one would think the woman behind the music was Norah Jones. Logan sat on one of the tall stools and ordered a chilled glass of Navan. She sipped the golden liquid slowly while she embraced the light sound of blues playing in the distance.

"Penny for your thoughts?" The older looking woman behind the bar waited patiently as long as she could before questioning the newcomer. Logan cracked a slight smile towards her. *Let's see, do I start with the dead bodies, screaming passengers, incompetent idiots, hot woman I've had extremely great sex with twice, or the stranger that appeared from my dreams?*

"I guess you could say life's been pretty hectic lately. I was due for a break."

"Ah...then I don't blame you honey. I'll be back with another round for you in just a minute."

"Thank you but that won't be necessary. I should be getting back to my hotel." Logan tossed a twenty on the counter next to her empty glass. On the way out of the bar she picked up her cell phone and dialed information.

"Los Angeles. I need the number for Chaney Steinen, please."

"I'm sorry ma'am there's no listing for that

name." Logan wrinkled her eyebrows for a second. *I know she changed...*"Wait ma'am can you please try Chaney Greer?"

"Yes here she is, four seven one, three two nine zero." Logan quickly dialed the number cursing herself for not saving it in her cell phone instead of her Palm Pilot. It rang a few times before a soft female voice answered.

"Did I wake you?"

"Logan? . . . Hey I saw you on the news, what a mess."

"Yeah, it's been pretty crazy. How are you?"

"Great. We had a late taping of the show; I just got home from the studio."

"That's good, how's the writing going?"

"It's all right. I've been trying out some new material. How long are you in town for?"

"I'm not sure right now. I'm working fourteen hour days and sleeping when I can find my hotel."

"That's insane. You're going to kill yourself one of these days working like that Logan."

"I know. I know, you always told me to slow down and here I am working harder than ever. I probably won't even make it back for Christmas or New Year's."

"I'm suppose to see my family for Hanukkah, I'm trying to rearrange my schedule so we'll see."

"I'll try to call you next week sometime. Maybe we can get together for a drink before I leave."

"Yeah, that sounds good; you should call my cell phone though. I usually never answer my home phone."

"I have your cell number at my hotel and I'm actually on my way from the airport so I called information. I thought you went back to using your maiden name?"

"I did, but for the sake of my bills and everything Greer is still my legal last name. I started using Steinen for my comedy and writing so I couldn't be looked up and I guess it's too late to change it now. Does it bother you?"

"No. Of course not."

Three

With the LAX disaster and ten other airport inspections behind her, Logan reclined on the soft couch in her Condo. She inhaled a salty breeze as it flowed in through the open French doors across from her. She smiled sweetly as she exhaled, delighted to finally be home. An irresponsible action at one of the largest American airports had caused an enormous uproar in the air travel industry. Five people lost their jobs and two more suspended due to negligence.

Logan's investigation confirmed a loss of pitch control due to a malfunctioning elevator control system caused the plane's nose to plunge to the ground after take off. The crash itself only had a simple malfunction to blame but, the loss of life could have been prevented if the proper inspections were being performed as scheduled. The fact that the airport administration broke down during a tragic emergency caused a few officials, including the ATC Chief of Operations to either lose their jobs or be suspended as well. It had taken Logan six long weeks to clean up the destructive mess. On top of that, she had to handle a week long private hearing in D.C. that brought the FAA up on safety violation charges.

Then, she continued traveling for three more weeks to finish the rest of her safety inspections throughout the country. Logan stopped her busy schedule long enough to phone the important people in her life and send Christmas presents to her family.

***

February rolled by before she knew it and Logan was headed to 'Jane's Place', happy to be working somewhat of a normal schedule again. Logan parked the truck close to the front door and strolled in. Out of the corner of her eye she noticed the person she thought she'd never see again. *Oh shit, here we go again.* Logan quickly made it to the bar and ordered a beer before the alluring blond was standing directly behind her.

A low husky voice whispered into her ear. "I haven't seen you in a while."

Logan turned to face the gray eyes piercing straight to her heart. Trying not to let her nerves take over, Logan quickly found the voice she was desperately searching for.

"I've been working...uh...a lot." *Why am I so damn nervous around her? What the hell Greer, get it together.*

"Dance with me." Jensen pulled Logan away from the bar and threaded her arms around her. Every inch of Logan's body was on fire, she couldn't let go of the softness in this woman's touch or the feeling of her own heart thrashing around in her chest. The song ended and Logan joined Jensen who headed back to her friends in the corner hogging the dartboard. Not one of the girls spoke to Logan. *What a bunch of assholes!* She tried hard to make small talk with Jensen but nothing seemed to go her way.

"So what do you do for a living?" Logan asked.

"If I told you, you wouldn't believe me."

"That's usually my line." Logan laughed, she felt like she was imposing since Jensen went right back to the game of Cricket that was interrupted when Logan entered the bar. Obviously her group of friends didn't like outsiders and Logan was clearly an outcast, so she walked back to the bar and ordered another beer.

"Logan, you know JT?" Bridgette, the bartender questioned jokingly.

"Nope. You?"

"She's my roommate."

Hmm...I hope you have better luck having a conversation with her. Logan chuckled and downed her beer.

Logan ran a hand threw her short locks as she put the key in the ignition of her truck. The nuisance gadget she carried in her pocket began vibrating and ringing that ridiculous Waltz tune that reminded her of the Addams Family. *Uh, not now. I just got home! Damn it!* Luckily the caller id read McCabe-FAA.

"Oh, I am not talking to you tonight. That's the last thing I need. Go talk to my voicemail Miss Thing!" She pushed the end button to stop the ringing. "I'm glad I put her in my phone otherwise I would've answered because of her damn Washington D.C. number."

***

Logan sat at her desk in black pants and a lavender blouse, reading the investigation manual changes and quarterly accident statistics that were just emailed to her. She stretched her neck and looked past her suit jacket hanging on the chair next to the large bay window that faced the runway, just in time to see a DC9 take off. *I'd kill for some Starbuck's, but I'm not walking across the airport.* A knock on the door extinguished that thought instantly. She spun her chair back around.

"Come in." A tall black man in a black and white TSA security uniform walked in. "Hey Ricky, how are you?"

"I'm good, a little cold out today, but I'd take that over the Florida heat any day." He smiled brightly. "I came up to tell you that the Sunshine Airlines passenger checked out okay."

"Thanks. You didn't have to come all the way up here, you know that."

"Yes, Ma'am, I was going to just tell Mr. Easton, but he wasn't answering his pages and he's not in his office."

"Yeah, I met with him this morning. I think he had a dentist appointment or something, he left earlier."

"I'd rather work than leave early to go to the dentist, and I'm in charge of the security in this terminal. I don't see a week shorter than sixty hours. But, I hate the dentist." He wrinkled his nose.

Logan smiled. "Believe, me Mr. Newton, *I know.*" They both laughed together.

***

Logan finished adding the new appendixes to her laptop in time to make it out of her office before eight o'clock. She grabbed her briefcase and headed towards the parking garage. "Hello Friday night! If I can make it through one weekend without any kind of call from Washington, I will bow down and kiss God's flip flops!"

"Excuse me?" Logan turned to find a well built man with dark hair and a thin mustache who could pass for a Ricky Martin look alike, dressed in a business suit starring wryly at her. "What did you just say?"

Opps. "I was…talking to myself."

"Out loud?" He smiled.

"Uh…yes that's correct. Do you mind?" She stepped around him and continued towards the employee parking floor of the garage. Of course, she heard footsteps behind her. "Look, I'm sorry if I offended you, but it's my right to freedom of speech. You can preach on someone else's doorstep. I really don't have time for it tonight."

The gentleman offered a hand to her. "I'm sorry I didn't get your name, I'm Matthew Taglia. I'm working here at the airport."

Logan looked at him and twisted her neck around pondering his face. "No you don't."

The handsome man laughed. "Yes I do, why would I lie to you?"

"I know just about everyone that works at this airport and I have never seen you until now."

"That would be because I just arrived today. I work for TSA Homeland Security." He flashed a TSA badge. "I'm on assignment from D.C."

Logan pulled her ID from her pocket and flashed her insignia. "I'm Agent Logan Greer."

"Well, it's nice to meet you, Agent Greer. Now I see why you want such a peaceful weekend."

Logan smiled. "Yes, and if you will please excuse

me Mr. Taglia, I'm late for an appointment."

"Please do excuse me Miss…uh…forgive me…Agent …Greer."

***

Logan sat on her couch nursing a chilled glass of Navan and listening to the waves crash against the shore. A sea-filled breeze blew in through the open French doors. What seemed like pure loneliness, was in fact, absolute tranquility. Logan finished her glass and sauntered into her room, immediately crashing onto her king-sized bed.

The alarm clock chimed loudly at eight o'clock. Thick satin sheets slid down uncovering average-sized, perfectly round breasts as the nude, suntanned blond sat straight up. "Damn stupid alarm clock!" Logan put on a dark blue sports bra, thin black panties, small gray shorts, and sneakers. She drank a glass of orange juice and programmed her feet to take her to the gym while she yawned.

***

Left, left…right…left, left…right…left, right, right…left…right…right…left.

"You're gonna kill yourself kid."

Logan stopped smacking the heavy bag and turned around. A short balding man with a snow-white colored mustache and goatee was looking at her.

"Did you say something?" She raised an eyebrow.

"Yeah, I see you here a lot beating the dog shit outta that bag. I can't tell who's winning, but you sure are putting up a good fight." He grinned, showing what appeared to be his real teeth, which were as pearly white as Logan's.

Logan smirked. "Well, I hope I'm winning," she laughed. "But, I'm not really keeping score."

The older man turned to walk away and looked back over his shoulder. "Just don't let that bag whip you."

The sweat glistened over bronze colored skin, soaking almost every strand of blond hair on Logan's head. She continued to pound the bag that swung in front of her for another hour. Logan quickly showered when she got back to her penthouse condo, changed into khaki shorts, a black tank top with the Hurley surf logo on the back and black sneakers with no socks. She put her badge fold in one back pocket and her cell phone in the other. *Cats Ass* roared to life as Logan piloted the beast down A1A.

The short ride was nice until she hit stop and go traffic close to the beach pavilion where the annual opening of the beaches festival was going on with live bands and vendor tents. Logan parked the Buell right up front next to the main entrance and walked straight to the beer line. She walked around stopping at a few of the vendors while drinking a long neck Bud Light since all they were serving was domestic beer.

She spotted Jensen, the blond woman of mystery thirty yards away starring a hole though her, wearing a white string bikini top and khaki shorts. Her curly blond hair hung loosely on her back just past her shoulders. *She's so adorable. Why the hell do I grow giant butterflies around her? I can let myself go completely with Brooke, but I can't even talk to this girl without fumbling.* Jensen walked towards Logan. A cute smile stretched across her face revealing flawless teeth. Jensen reached up and pushed Logan's sunglasses up on her head. *For god's sake don't look down Greer.*

"You shouldn't hide those gorgeous eyes." A sultry voice floated out of the young looking woman. Logan cleared her throat, in need of words, some sort of goddamn words. *Say something to her Logan you goof!*

"Hi." *Lovely, you idiot. You are intelligent, a damn aeronautical science engineer and you say hi?*

Jensen laughed and shook her head. "Hi yourself."

"So, are you planning on staying all day?"

"Yeah, I'm here with some friends. You?"

"I doubt it. My friend's band is playing soon. After that I'll probably go home. I don't live far from here and it looks like it might rain."

"Did you walk?"

"No I rode my motorcycle. I just washed and waxed it so I'll be pissed if it rains before I get it back in the garage."

"I should get back to my friends. It was nice talking to you again."

"Wait…" Logan was tired of the game of cat and mouse. *This is the longest conversation…the only conversation you've ever had with her. Don't blow it!* "Can I call you sometime?"

"Two Four One, Six Six One Six." Jensen spoke nonchalantly and disappeared into the crowd just as quickly as she had appeared. Logan programmed the number in her phone and finished her beer while she listened to an awesome blues band with a lead singer that could melt a slide guitar with her fingers. When the music ended a young woman about Logan's size, with shoulder length black hair and tan skin, jumped off of the stage and walked over to her. A thick raspy voice came out as she spoke.

"Hey, babe." She leaned in and kissed Logan on the cheek.

"Hey, you sounded great!"

"Yeah, I was using my new slide, I love it. So whatcha been up to? I never hear from you or see your ass out anymore."

"I know, I just got back in town not too long ago. I've been really busy with work."

"Still playin' with the airplanes, huh."

"Oh yeah. I'll never give it up. It's like a drug addiction."

"Haha, sounds like me with music. At least you make a hell of a lot more money than I do."

"I never hear you complaining though."

"Nope, 'cause it's a drug! Haha. Hey so I saw you talking to Jensen. Did she bite you too?"

"Bite me? Lynnie what the hell are you talking about?"

"I used to talk to her. She tried to pull me away from Rachel when we were dating last year. That chick is seriously twisted watch out."

"Gotcha. She hasn't done much to me."

"Yet!" Lynnie added.

"Haha, one can only hope." Logan wiggled her eyebrows.

"She's hot, but she bites."

"Mm, I like it."

Lynnie smacked Logan on the arm. "Crazy, come on let me by you a beer."

"Sure, I never turn down a cold one."

"You'd shoot Tequila with me if you weren't such a puss." Lynnie chided.

"Please, you know I can handle it, I just don't like the taste."

"Once again…puss!"

"Yeah, yeah, yeah."

"Hey did you ride?"

"You know it. Where do you wanna go?"

"Hmm, let's go to your place."

"Nice try, you can flirt with me all you want Lynnie, but it'll never happen." Both women laughed. "Seriously, can you get out of here or do you need to hang around?"

"Nah, I can leave. Let's go to Joe's Crab Shack, I'm fucking starving."

"You're always starving, girl, you eat more than both of us together." Lynnie snickered. "So where did you park the cat?"

***

Monday morning came around all too soon. At six o'clock a.m. Logan was in Terminal A waiting for her plane to Washington, D.C. to take off. She had an early meeting with her boss at the NTSB headquarters and an afternoon meeting with the FAA Major Investigation Office to review the safety recommendations that the NTSB gave them ninety-days ago following the LAX accident.

Logan was on her way to the parking area to catch a cab after her plane landed, when she heard a man's voice and turned to see who was calling for her.

48

"Hello there, Agent Greer, what brings you to my part of the country?" The tall, dark, and handsome man asked. Logan recognized him immediately.

"Mr. Taglia." She nodded her hello. "I'm here for meetings all day," she said flatly. He smiled in return.

"Did you ever get that peaceful weekend that you were hoping for?"

"No."

"I know what you mean. I have a hectic schedule myself. Try living up here."

"They couldn't pay me enough." Both of them laughed.

Once outside of Dulles, Logan hailed a taxi.

"I'm going to Four Ninety L'Enfant Plaza South West."

***

Logan sat at the oval shaped table in the dark blue office, admiring the NTSB seal that covered the entire wall in front of her. Being in that building was not as nerve racking as it had been the first few times she was there. She did not get to her position by being shy or nervous.

Her meeting with Walter Hudson, her boss and Head of the Aviation Board, went rather well as expected. Her next meeting was the one bothering her nerves. Auditing the FAA was always a pain in the ass, especially when it was because of an accident that could have been prevented. That meant she'd have to sit with the NTSB Air Safety Coordinator and listen to him yell because more than likely they hadn't even started the safety recommendation list that was suppose to be completed and signed off on two weeks ago.

Back in a taxi, she spit out another address and handed the man a twenty, while the Air Safety Coordinator sat next to her going over his notes.

"Eight Hundred, Independence Avenue South West, please."

As she predicted, she sat at the large table listening to the older man yell at five FAA agents, including the beautiful Brooke McCabe, dressed in a black business suit with her long hair pulled back in a bun. She had Logan's attention during the entire two hours. Ironically, most of the orders had been completed so Logan didn't have to get too loud when it was her turn to talk to them. She left the ASC and decided to go find a hotel for the night since she had a last minute meeting scheduled for the next morning. Logan was practically running through the exit doors of the FAA building when her cell phone began vibrating in her pocket.

Washington, it figures, what now.

"Agent Greer," Logan answered.

A sweet and innocent sounding voice was on the other end. "Are you running from me?"

"No, of course not, Miss McCabe."

"Cut the Miss McCabe shit, my name is Brooke."

"I know what your name is. I'm trying to be professional." *It's really hard to work around you and not think of your sensually beautiful skin against me. I can't remember the last time I had extremely hot sex before I met you. You set my body on fire.*

"Loosen up Greer. You're panties are tighter than a nun's...never mind. Where are you? You left in such a hurry."

"I'm on the way to my hotel. I was supposed to be headed home, but nothing ever goes as planned when it comes to D.C."

"You can say that again. What hotel are you staying in?"

"Why?"

"I want to see you."

"That's not a good idea." *I want to see you too. I need to see you. I shouldn't see you.*

"You've never had a problem with seeing me before."

"I …I'm staying at the Adams Mark, room Seven Twenty Two."

***

Two hours later Logan sat in her upscale hotel room staring at the wall…alone. As usual, she had spent the time of her life rolling around the sheets with the beautiful seductress. "I swear I don't understand it. Here I am talking to my damn self…ugh…women!" She had asked Brooke to stay the night with her, not expecting to be shot down.

"Stay with me…"

"I can't, I'm sorry."

"No one knows you're here."

"Yeah, and it'll stay that way…if I leave now."

"This is crazy Brooke…"

"No strings…remember?"

"Yeah…I know…it just…sometimes it seems like a booty call or some shit." Brooke put both hands on Logan's face and then ran a hand through the thick, short blond hair.

51

"It has never felt like that...for me."

"I didn't say it felt like it, I meant it resembles one, that's all."

"I'll call you. Have a safe flight home."

Brooke left as quickly as she had arrived.

Logan decided not to spend anymore time trying to figure out what had occurred and the reason behind it.

A week later, Logan was standing on her balcony stargazing and listening to the ocean. *Call her. The phone won't dial itself.* "Why the hell do I get so freaked out over this girl? I have never been like this, what the hell is wrong with me?" She stepped inside and grabbed her cell phone from the kitchen counter, dialing the saved number. When the voice prompted, she left a short message to say hi and give her number in return. As soon as she closed the phone, it began ringing in her hand.

"Hey Lynnie, I was just thinking about you, I was getting ready to put *Lynnie and the Boyz* in the CD player. What's up?"

"Hey babe, I'm actually in town with a free Saturday night. Wanna meet me for a drink? I can sing to you live." She giggled.

"What bar are you going to?"

"I was thinking 'Hairy Larry's'. There won't be anyone there that I know, except for Larry, if he's even around. I haven't played there in forever, he's probably pissed at me. Hmm,...any suggestions?"

"Let's go somewhere within walking distance for me. I feel like stumbling down the beach tonight."

"Isn't there a new martini bar down there at the end of the boardwalk? How far is that from you?"

"Not far, you know I live in The Ocean's Reef

Luxury Condo's. I think that place is called Martini Palace or some shit like that. It's at the end of the strip of Condo's before you get to the restaurants next to the new Irish Pub on the corner. You'll have to park on one of the side streets somewhere. We only have a few visitor parking spots, and they're usually occupied all weekend."

"No sweat, I'll meet you in ten minutes out front of your building."

***

Logan met Lynnie and walked the five or so blocks down to the bar. Both women were wearing loose jeans and flip flops. Lynnie had on a tight camouflage t-shirt and Logan was in a baby blue t-shirt. The young looking, red-headed bartender came right over as the girls sat down. She spoke with a squeaky cartoon voice. Lynnie almost choked trying not to laugh.

"What can I get for you two?"

"Are you drinking beer?" Logan asked. Lynnie just nodded.

"A Bud Light and a Killian's please."

"I'll need to see both of your ID's." Lynnie showed hers first, then Logan flashed her picture, trying to hide the emblem on the other side of the bi-fold style badge cover.

"So how's the music business these days?"

Lynnie took a long swallow of her beer and turned towards her friend. "It's crazy, I never know whether I'm coming or going. We just booked a new Southeast tour from Louisiana across to Georgia and Florida."

"Wow, that's great!"

"Yeah but its thirty bars or events in sixty days. I wont be able to speak, much less move when I get back."

"I know how it is, sometimes I wonder if I even slept the night before. Hell, I've literally had weeks go by and not realize it."

"Damn, I didn't think airplanes were that much of a pain in the ass."

"The plane is never the problem, Ninety percent of the time it's the people that work on it or the idiot that's flying it."

"So you basically fly around and check up on the airports all over the country?"

"Well, amongst other things, yes." Logan never told anyone except her family and her ex-wife about her being a Government Agent and the details to her job. Lynnie knew she worked for the government dealing with airplanes, but not much else. "Have you been in the studio lately? I'm looking forward to some new music."

"We're working on a new album. I want it finished before the road tour, but Corey is taking his sweet ass time trying to get us a recording schedule. Who knows?"

"Hey, guess who was asking about you the other night. I went to that weird lesbian bar you go to, they keep calling me to play there…"

"And…who the hell was asking about me up there?"

"Jensen, a.k.a. snake in the grass." Logan spit her beer all over the counter in surprised laughter.

"That's odd. What did she want?" One blond eyebrow rose up as she waited.

"She was asking how well I knew you and if you were dating anyone."

"And…"

"That was it. I was on my way out."

"What did you say to her?" Lynnie ran her hand through her shoulder length thick dark hair and grinned. "Lynnie!"

"Ha-ha you're pissing your pants over this chick. She's not worth it, trust me she's a player, ask any girl in that bar. Anyway, I told her we were pretty good friends and as far as I knew you were single. You *are* single right?"

"Of course, I haven't been in a relationship since Chaney and I were married. You know that. I've dated but nothing serious enough to call it anything."

"Speaking of Chaney, how is she? I saw her show on TV not too long ago. She's hilarious!"

"Yeah, I saw her a few weeks ago when I was in L.A. working. She's doing really well and dating some new girl."

"That's cool, does it bother you to see her or see her with someone else?"

"No. I mean I miss her a lot because we use to be inseparable, but it's been almost three years. I never have seen her serious with anyone. I have met a couple of the girls that she has dated when I've been in town and hung out with her. It's not a big deal. We'll always love each other. We're just happier apart, you know."

"Yeah."

"Hey speaking of Jensen, I called her earlier and she never returned my call."

"Send her a text message; she's all into that shit." Logan pulled out her phone and entered …*Hey just wanted to see if you got my message.* Immediately her phone lit up.

"See."

"Hmm…"

"Well?"

"She got the message and wants to know what I'm doing." Logan invited Jensen to join her for a drink, but she refused, saying she was out with some friends.

***

Logan and Jensen continued to text message each other off and on for another two weeks since Jensen never answered her phone nor did she return a voicemail. Their conversations usually were just to say hey. Logan asked her a few times to meet up for a drink or go to dinner and the other woman always refused, making an excuse that she had either just gotten in from work, had to be up early for work, or just plain didn't feel like going out. They never spoke of their jobs or anything else about themselves for that matter. The only facts that Logan knew about her were, she was twenty-six, lived in an apartment with the bartender from the lesbian bar, originally from Illinois, and she had a bachelor's degree in something to do with science. She acted reclusive and very similar to Logan when it came to her own life.

Four

Logan was sound asleep, buried under a mountain of satin sheets, pillows, and a comforter. At five thirty a.m. her cell phone began rumbling a high pitch ridiculous sound. Logan shot out from under the heap above her as if her ass was on fire. Eyes still closed, she flipped the gadget open.

"Greer!"

"Hello, Agent Greer, this is Cole Donovan, NTSB-Washington."

"Yes, I know who you are."

"I just received word that a major airliner went down in Jacksonville."

"What! Oh my god! Where? What area?"

"I'm not sure yet Ma'am. This was reported to me within two minutes ago." Logan stumbled out of her bed and into the closet searching for some sort of clothing to cover her nude form.

"I believe it was in a wooded clearing near JIA. That's all I can confirm as of right now."

"Son of a bitch! I mean…"

"I know…head towards the airport and I'll let you know as soon as I have something else to go on."

***

The black Sport Trac was moving close to ninety miles per hour up 9-A North. As soon as she hit I-295 North she turned the truck down Lem Turner Road. The smoke from the fire was mixing with the clouds overhead as the sun began rising. *There you are.* The entrance to the wooded area was lit up with hundreds of flashing lights. Logan immediately called the Washington Office to relay the coordinates and let her team know she was on scene. The minute she stepped from the truck three Police officers were on her with their guns pointed at her nose. She carefully nodded towards the badge that was attached to her belt much like a police detective's.

"If you gentlemen and lady would like to keep your jobs, I suggest you put your toys away." Logan was dressed in jeans with her gun tucked in its holster under her familiar black polo shirt with the NTSB logo on the left front breast, 'IIC' stitched on the other side, and black Doc Marten shoes on her feet. She pushed past the cops and ran up to what appeared to be an airplane shredded to pieces and burning with flames higher than the tree line. The fire department worked vigorously trying to detain the fire. Logan was the only 'official' on scene; this turned a hectic situation into complete chaos. She was being pulled in fifty different directions, finally she snapped. Logan climbed up onto a large fragment of metal that resembled the left wing and started yelling at the top of her lungs.

"Alright people, I'm only going to say this once. I'm Agent Logan Greer, the Investigator In Charge with the National Transportation Board. I am the *only* one commanding this operation! The only people I want to see within two hundred yards of that wreckage is the fire department personnel, all others will be restrained by the police department or me personally. Is that understood...Good. At this moment, my team has been notified and they are on their way as I speak. By the looks of this mess, there are no survivors so our only option is to get the fire out and leave the wreckage intact for the investigation. This is 'official' evidence people. Do not touch anything unless I tell you to. At this time I would like this half of the police officers to spread out a hundred yards and secure the area, this half needs to go out another hundred pass them and do not allow anyone to get passed you. No press, no airport staff, no one means no one! I suggest you write this number down...four, four, two, six, eight, seven, two, this is my cell number. If anyone is asking to come near here, you call me. If someone gets past you guys and gets to me without authorization I promise I will have your ass. Is all of this clear to everyone? Good."

She jumped down and went over to towards the largest piece, which looked as though it could be the front half of the fuselage. The smell was almost as horrendous as the sight. Metal scraps torn to bits, wires ripped apart, interior seating burnt beyond recognition, bodies charred to ashes. She could make out a shoe here or a piece of jewelry there as she shined the flashlight around. *My god...*She put her right hand on her forehead and then ran it through her hair. *What a mess. Those poor souls never stood a chance in this twisted inferno.*

She always dreaded having to sift through the corpses or what was left of them and crawl around in the remains of the wreckage. Logan tumbled out of a severed part of the second section of the fuselage as her phone fluttered wildly in her pocket. Her blond hair and tanned skin were covered with a mix of soot and fluids. She wiped clean as much as she could.

"Greer!"

"Uh...this is Officer Sutton, I have a few people here that say they are with you."

"I need names Sutton, give me some names!" She pulled the list out of her pocket, of investigators and specialists for the NTSB and FAA that were emailed to her laptop. The officer hurriedly checked their ID's and Logan allowed them all to enter.

"Um...the Mayor is here too."

"Tell him I'll be with him in ten minutes."

***

Her team arrived with the FAA hot on their heels. Logan led them to an area where they could set up the 'official' tents and communication lines running on generators, amongst other equipment. She walked to the front of the group, vigorously wiping the crud from her face and hands. She barely recognized her usually seductive, beautiful alter ego, dressed in jeans and a yellow t-shirt with FAA in bold letters across the back. She had gray colored sneakers on her feet, and her long hair was twisted tightly into a bun. *She looks so sweet and innocent, definitely younger.*

"Listen up everyone. I'm sure you all know the specifics, this pile use to be a Boeing 737... East Coast Airlines, Flight 1792 Charlotte to Jacksonville... 120 casualties, including the pilot, co-pilot, and two flight attendants. I was on scene within thirty minutes of the call to Washington. As you can see most of the fire has been extinguished, except for the remaining jet fuel that's covering most of the ground on the other side of the wreckage. I've been through both tattered portions of the fuselage." She took a deep breath trying to lose the pictures in her mind.

"We're past the rescue stage, it's time to move on to the recovery and try to put this hodgepodge back into some sort of order. Everyone needs to spread out and start collecting any and every scrap of this airplane that you can find. Remember to take pictures and mark every spot with GPS coordinates and a flag. I'll need the Human Factors Specialists to come with me so we can begin removing the human remains. Okay. We all know how to 'tag 'n bag' evidence, let's get to it. Here's the two way radio's, make sure everyone gets one. I'm on channel twelve, call me with any and all questions. As for you guys with the FAA, your IIC is on channel ten if you can't get a hold of me. Do not speak to anyone on these grounds except myself. Now if you will excuse me, the Mayor is about to flip out on our Police Barricade."

Logan looked like she'd been through hell and back. She stretched her neck and back while running a hand through her short hair trying not to look as rough as she felt. She began walking towards her truck when she heard a soft voice behind her and sensed the most wonderful, flower-like scent she had ever smelled, a scent she was very familiar with.

"How are you?"

"Better than I look." Logan smiled wryly as she turned around.

"I hope so, you look like shit."

"Thank you Simon, where did you hide Paula and Randy? I'd like to hear everyone's opinion, please, come on...let's..." The smaller woman nonchalantly grabbed

Logan's hand.

"Hey...calm down I think your roughed up look is kind of sexy actually. Plus, I just wanted to make sure you were okay, I know you've been crawling around in that clutter, probably when the damn thing was still in flames." Logan snickered and stared into Brooke's green eyes. "I've missed seeing you."

"Yeah, me too."

***

That evening Logan had changed into a black pants suit with a canary yellow blouse under her jacket. The press conference at the airport, along with the meeting with the Mayor and Governor had only taken about two hours of her time. She was grateful since she'd rather be on scene heading up the investigation instead of playing politics with a bunch of men on power trips.

Her supervisor had authorized a hotel room for her since her condo was a good distance away in Jacksonville Beach, but Logan insisted on going home to her comfortable bed. *It will be hell or high water before I will stay in a hotel in my own city.*

Logan had asked Brooke to meet her for dinner but she was trying to get settled into a hotel and take care of some paperwork that needed to be faxed to her home office so Logan raided the refrigerator and stretched out in bed with a glass of Navan to watch a late movie that she had already missed the first half hour of. Her mind wandered off as she fell asleep on the comfortable sofa.

***

Logan was back on the scene at six a.m. Most of her team was arriving right behind her. Brooke rode over from the nearby airport Clarion Hotel with some of the FAA team. Logan stepped over to the 'official' tent with four containers of Starbucks coffee consisting of various flavors.

"You guys can fight over these and I picked this up for the rest of you." She took a sip of her own Mocha and tossed one of the guys a bag of Starbucks coffee grounds for the machines on the table. Brooke was nearby talking on her radio to one of her specialists. Logan grabbed the last coffee and took it over to her.

"Morning." *Sexy royal pain in my ass!*

"Hey there." Brooke examined the business suit Logan was wearing, winked in acceptance, and licked her lips slowly. "You look just as good peeled out of that suit."

Logan took a deep breath, fighting back the waterfall between her legs. *You can peel me out of it anytime.* "We have a meeting this morning with the FBI. They always stick their nose in everything, you know that."

"Yeah, I hate dealing with them. Are you ready?" Brooke asked as she sipped her coffee.

***

Their meeting was brief and to the point. So far, there was no evidence of foul play or a terrorist attack. Therefore, the FBI was not needed. Brooke and Logan made that pretty clear. As soon as they were back at the site Logan was called on the radio.

"Who is trying to get out here?"

The officer repeated himself. "The ID says J. Tirado, Environmental Field Supervisor, Environmental Protection Agency."

"Who the hell..." *EPA...shit.* "Let him in."

"Uh...it's a her, ma'am."

"Okay...let *her* in." *Who gives two shits!*

***

Logan was standing in the 'official' tent going over the cockpit schematics of the aircraft. Most of the plane debris was being moved slowly into a private hangar at JIA. The NTSB and FAA teams were gathering the last of the data and photographing the area. Brooke was facing Logan, they were discussing one of the documents that needed to be faxed, when she noticed Logan's blue-green eyes grow as round as baseballs and turn dark blue.

Brooke turned to see a woman with curly blond hair pulled back behind her head, dressed in jeans and a white polo shirt. She was roughly Brooke's height, which was still three inches shorter than Logan. Brooke thought this woman looked young, she was built more athletic than dainty like herself, very cute, and staring back at Logan like she was a ghost, with the same deer in the headlights look.

"Am I missing something? Who are you?" Brooke spat out. The younger looking woman snapped out of the stare and stepped over to the tent.

"I'm looking for the person in charge." Logan stepped around Brooke.

"I...I'm in charge here, Agent Logan Greer with the National Transportation Safety Board. You must be..."

"Jensen Tirado, I'm a field supervisor for the Jacksonville EPA, this is Kevin, he's one of my field workers." She nodded towards a brown-haired man about two inches taller than Logan's five foot-five inch frame.

"Why didn't you ever tell me what you did?" Logan asked quietly.

Jensen shrugged her shoulders. "No one ever believes me anyway, besides you're the one with the hot shot job. Why didn't you tell me?"

Logan stood her ground firmly. "That's precisely why. I don't need the world knowing I'm a government agent. It's not as thrilling as it sounds."

Brooke stepped between the two, ready to slap them both.

"I take it you two know each other?"

"Yeah, sort of." Logan's eyebrows furled together. "I was told you guys would be stopping by. What exactly is it that you are going to do?"

"We're Environmental Scientist. We test the soil when there's a pollution hazard to the environment. I'm the Field Supervisor, so I get called when it's something major."

"I see, well follow me. The majority of the jet fuel was spilled over there." Logan walked them to the area that was still saturated. "Here we are, do not touch anything except the dirt." Jensen laughed and rolled her eyes. "I'm not joking, this is an investigation and as far as I'm concerned you two are tampering with evidence."

Jensen stepped closer than she should have and looked straight at Logan's face with her soft gray eyes. She opened her mouth to let a quiet whisper escape. "I promise not to touch *anything*, unless you ask me to."

She winked as she backed away. Logan's breath caught in her throat causing her to cough. She walked back to the communication area, she noticed Brooke piercing her with a razor sharp stare.

"What the hell was that all about?"

"What?"

"You know what. So, what's going on between you and *miss mad scientist*?"

Logan brushed some dirt off of her suit jacket and simply answered the question.

"Nothing, nada, zilch. Why? Does it bother you?"

"Nope."

"Good. Now that that's covered, I have some work to get done here before I go over to the hangar."

Brooke shook her head and walked in the opposite direction, keeping one eye on the little adversary at all times.

Three hours later, Logan was eating a sandwich and talking to Washington on her cell phone. Jensen walked up behind her. Logan heard her coming from a few feet away and turned to face her sneak attacker as she hung up her phone.

"Can I help you?" Her nerves were beginning to take over.

"Nah, I was just coming here to talk to you."

"Okay, you have my attention." *Be calm Greer.*

"Do I? By the looks of it I'd say that hottie in the skirt suit over there has it. She's been chopping me to bits with her eyes all morning."

Logan didn't have to turn around; she knew what 'hottie' Jensen was referring to. *What a cluster fuck.*

"That's Brooke McCabe, she's an investigator with the FAA. Her bark is bigger than her bite. So, what's up? Did you guys find out anything?"

"I won't know until we get everything back to the lab, but it looks pretty bad. It hasn't rained much this year so the soil really soaked up the jet fuel."

"That's not good, at least the fire didn't spread to the forest line." Logan felt the butterflies in her stomach begin to settle.

"That's true…" She couldn't help laughing as she inspected the sharp dressed woman in front of her.

"Hey, what's so funny?" Logan's face tightened.

"I can't get over the outfit and the title for that matter. It's really weird, I'm use to…"

"Seeing me as a girl in the bar wearing flip flops, a t-shirt, and jeans."

"Something like that, I had no idea you had a job like this. I only saw part of the accident. It gave me chills and turned my stomach."

"Yeah, it's definitely not an easy profession by any means, but it's my calling, and has been ever since I was a little kid I've loved being around airplanes. I would actually spend hours reading the research on what caused the accident's and so on."

"Hmm…"

"By the way, why didn't you ever call me?"

"You always text me."

"That's because you never answer your phone."

Jensen winked and smiled shyly. "Maybe next time I will."

"I'll hold you to it then." Logan smiled back.

"You do that."

***

Later that afternoon Brooke watched as Logan drove Jensen and her partner back to their vehicle at the front of the Police Barricade. She waved as they went by with her teeth clenched so tightly she thought her jaw would break. Jensen briefly hugged Logan and told her it was good to see her again, too bad it was on unfortunate circumstances. Logan didn't want to release the smaller woman, but she was on professional terms with her at this point. Although, the lingering scent left in the air drove her senses over the edge as the mystifying woman walked away. Logan sensed the upcoming confrontation with 'Her Highness' at the crash site, and decided to go over to the hangar instead to finish a few more grueling hours of reports that had to be completed before the end of her day.

Logan managed to slip away from Brooke and keep herself busy for the next two days. Brooke finally caught up to her as Logan was on her way to her truck, glad that it was finally Friday. She had worked straight through to eight o'clock and was ready to be away from the airport. She was happy to see Brooke heading her way, but not in the mood for jealousy over someone that she herself barely knew.

"Hey, why are you hiding from me?"

"I'm not hiding. I've been busy and I don't need the FAA up my ass all day long."

"Whoa, excuse me. I didn't know you felt like that about me. I will definitely finish my work and be out of here soon, so you don't have to worry about the FAA anymore." Brooke snapped back before turning to walk away.

"Wait." Brooke began walking in the opposite direction before Logan spoke.

"Damn it McCabe turn around." When the woman showed no sign of stopping Logan ran up behind her.

"Look, I'm sorry. You're the one who overreacted with the EPA people and made yourself look like an ass. I don't know what's going on with you. Hell, for that matter I don't know even you Brooke. We meet up, sleep together, and leave. Then, I hear from you once in a blue moon until I see you again. I damn sure didn't think we were serious, if you did then I'm sorry. I tried to see you and you wouldn't allow it. For the record, I do know Jensen, and I have been talking to her for a while. Nothing's going on between us. I shouldn't have to explain myself to you."

Brooke stood still, biting her lip in mute silence. Logan was beyond pissed at this woman.

"You're absolutely right. You don't have to explain anything to me. I guess it was all a misunderstanding. I really do not want to fight with you over something this stupid, especially when I can be doing something else to you right about now."

Brooke grabbed Logan's hand.

"Uh…"

"Where are you parked?"

Logan pointed to the black truck a few feet away.

Brooke smiled, and took a quick glance around the parking lot. Satisfied that no one was watching she leaned forward and kissed Logan's soft lips, lingering for a second to taste her warm lips before pulling away.

"Take me home with you." Brooke whispered seductively. Logan smiled and obeyed the enchanting woman in front of her. *Why do I always give in to her?*

***

69

Brooke couldn't believe her eyes when they stepped off of the elevator on the Penthouse floor. Logan unlocked the door, swung it open and smiled as she waved Brooke to enter first. The smaller woman was amazed as she walked through the tile foyer and into the spacious living area of the gorgeous, very modernly decorated condo. Logan took her hand and gave her the presidential tour. They started at the first room off of the foyer.

"This is the guest room." Across from that was an entrance to a hallway where she saw a second room used as a gym, a large bathroom and at the end of the hallway was the master bedroom. Logan led Brooke into her room, where she had a black and silver king-sized sleigh bed with matching furniture. The walk-in closet was behind the entire wall on the left side, across from that was a set of French doors that led to the balcony, which gave a magnificent view of the beach and ocean. Opposite of the bed was the gigantic bathroom with a marble garden-spa tub, matching double sinks, a fully enclosed glass shower with double heads, and of course a toilet in the corner. Logan smiled on the inside as she watched Brooke admiring her home.

"Come on there's more." She led Brooke out of the hallway and back to the foyer that led to the open kitchen that looked out over the living area. Stainless steel appliances blended perfectly with the marbled counter tops and dark wooden cabinets. Another set of French doors led from the breakfast nook to the balcony. They walked down the three small steps into the living area, There was a fireplace along the wall, a sectional sofa, and marble tables with glass tops. A flat screen plasma television was on the wall in the corner. Another set of French doors lead out to the balcony and the fresh ocean air. Behind the couch was a study that had matching French doors as its entry.

"This is my office." Logan showed Brooke her massive desk and matching bookcase. Along the walls were different newspaper articles and pictures of Major Airline investigations that Logan had been assigned to, from her very first investigation as a specialist to her first one as Investigator In Charge. Next to those were about a half dozen certifications, a Bachelors Degree and a Masters Degree. Beside those hung a small case on the wall with what appeared to be military medals with a young picture of her at the top and a picture of a man at the bottom. Next to that was a large framed Family Crest complete with the Motto, History, and Coat of Arms Insignia. The bookcase on the other side held a few pictures and different die-cast models of airplanes and NASA Space Shuttles. Brooke looked closely at the photos on the shelf. They appeared to be different family pictures and one that appeared to be a wedding picture, the other woman in the picture with Logan was also in a few of the other pictures as well. Brooke turned back towards Logan with a confused look on her face.

"That's Chaney. She's my ex-wife. She lives in L.A." Logan said.

"She's beautiful." Brooke looked closely at the photo's of the woman that seemed to be slightly shorter than Logan, with long curly black hair.

"I swear I have seen her before."

"You probably have. She's an actress and a comedian with her own sitcom."

"Wow, that's awesome. Do you still talk to her?"

"Yeah, we were always best friends. I saw her while I was at LAX for that accident not long ago. I talk to her probably every other month or so."

"If you don't mind my asking…"

"No, please ask away."

"How long were you married?"

"We were together eight years and married for the last four. We've been divorced for about three years."

"That's a long time with the same person."

"We were happy, our careers pulled us apart. She went to L.A. and I went to D.C. and we couldn't make the distance thing work. After I became an IIC I moved back here and bought this place. It was too late for me and her by that time, so we divorced and vowed to stay friends and continue to be a part of each others life."

Brooke felt her heart leap from her chest towards this woman. She walked back towards the Family Crest and Military Medals.

"What's this for?"

"It's my family's, we're from Scotland. My Mother and Father moved to the States and had me. The rest of my family lives outside of the main land."

"Wow, that's definitely different."

"Is there anything else that you want to know?" Logan asked.

"Not unless there's anything else that you want to tell me." Brooke pulled Logan against her and ran her hands under the taller woman's suit jacket. She felt the gun tucked snuggly in its holster. "Why do you carry this?"

Logan flinched and backed away from Brooke. She took a deep breath, searching for a subject change. *Talking about Chaney is nothing compared to that. How*

72

can I tell her? I'm surprised she doesn't already know. I guess no one told her who I was. Props to the FAA for not exposing me. She laughed on the inside.

"Come on." Logan grabbed Brooke's hand and walked her back into the living room. "I'll be right back." She went into her room and hung her jacket in the closet and placed her gun, still in its holster, on the nightstand by her bed. The lean, tanned figure changed into khaki shorts and a baby blue colored Polo shirt. She left her feet bare and walked out into the main area of the condo where Brooke was sitting on the couch.

"Mm, you look sexy in shorts." Brooke stood up in time to catch Logan trying to walk past her. She stopped Logan in her tracks as she ran her hand up one smooth skinned leg and into the opening of the shorts. Logan backed away slowly.

"Aren't you hungry?" Logan questioned jokingly.

Brooke answered with the most lust driven look that Logan had ever seen.

"I'm hungry for you," she said huskily.

Logan pulled Brooke into an intense kiss, lips parting passionately allowing tongues to taste and explore slowly at first. Both women were undressing each other between kisses as they made their way to the bedroom. Logan opened the French doors to let in the moonlight and the salt air.

Finally out of their clothes, both women laid down in the satin sheets. They tenderly kissed every inch of each other's body and caressed one another as they slowly made love together for the first time. Neither one admitted the passionate feeling, but both women felt the adoration that passed between them.

Brooke awoke, alone as the sun rose in her face.

Logan had shut the doors but left the curtains pulled apart to allow the light to enter the room. Brooke twisted her long hair into a bun behind her head and walked out of the bedroom, her nude skin glowing in the sunlight. She found a note on the counter in the kitchen.

Good Morning,

I went down to the gym. I should be back around 8 or so. You looked so peaceful sleeping, I didn't want to wake you and I couldn't sleep any longer. I'll see you soon! Logan

***

Brooke smiled and took it upon herself to rummage through the refrigerator. Logan arrived on time. She was caught off guard as she walked into her condo. Brooke was in the kitchen cooking naked. Logan's jaw was on the floor and her eyes were bulging out of her head. *My god this woman is unbelievably sexy.*

"Hey, you're just in time. I hope you like pancakes. I figured they were pretty neutral since I have no idea what you eat."

Logan smiled and leaned in to kiss the fascinating woman in front of her.

"I think pancakes will do just fine." She laughed.

Both women enjoyed their breakfast while looking out at the ocean. Logan put everything in the dishwasher and pulled Brooke's nude form against her. She ran her tongue between two firm round breasts and up towards an adorable ear lobe. Before she could speak, Brooke's hands were under her sports bra. Logan bent slightly and scooped up the delicate woman with no problem. She maneuvered her way into the master bedroom and deposited Brooke next to the glass shower door. Quickly, Brooke helped Logan out of her workout clothes.

The water was hot and rapidly steamed up the glass around them. Logan kissed her way down to the honey colored curls, lapping her tongue between the folds around Brooke's clit as Brooke grabbed her shoulders for leverage.

"Ahh…yeah right there…" Brooke moaned and pulled Logan's wet head harder against her. Logan stood up. Backing Brooke against the wall, she inserted two fingers easily inside the wetness. She moved slowly in and out, as she felt the muscles around her tighten she went deeper and faster. The water rushed over the women from both shower heads while their mouths met with passionate force as they licked lips and sucked tongues.

Brooke tensed one last time in Logan's arms before she went limp with a soft moan. It only took mere seconds for the smaller woman to regain her strength. Brooke leaned forward claiming a taut nipple between her teeth as Logan let out a tiny yelp. She didn't stop there, Brooke ran one hand up into Logan's short hair, pulling lightly, while her other hand made it's way down to the sweet spot between Logan's legs. Brooke rubbed the engorged clit back and forth, then in circles. Finally, she entered her with one swift motion. Penetrating harder and then slow and easy until the taller woman cried out with pleasure and pulled Brooke tightly into her arms. They stayed glued together for what seemed like minutes, then, released each other to bathe and wash one another's hair.

Outside of the shower Brooke realized she didn't have anything with her except for the skirt suit that she was wearing the night before.

"Um…I should've thought this out. I think." She laughed.

"I'm not much bigger than you, I'm sure I have something around here that you can put on. Be my guest." Logan waved around the closet.

A few minutes later Brooke came out wearing jeans that were a size too big and a white surf logo t-shirt. Ironically, Logan was dressed similar, except her shirt was black.

"Don't you look cute!" Logan snickered as she grabbed the smaller woman and kissed her, slightly picking her up off of the floor.

"You have good taste, look at you." They both chuckled.

"So, what's your plan for today, Sherlock?"

Logan appeared to be deep in thought for a moment.

"Ah, my dear beautiful Watson, you see I was hoping you would join me for a ride on the Cat's Ass." Logan began talking with a thick Scottish accent.

"A what!? Excuse me…"

Logan continued the accent. "Oh silly me, I meant a motorbike ride."

Brooke looked confused as hell. Logan giggled and cut out the accent.

"My motorcycle, her name is Cat's Ass. I was hoping you would like to take a ride with me."

"I…uh…sure. I had no idea you had a motorcycle. Where are we going?"

"That's a surprise. Come on you'll need some shoes."

Fate Vs. Destiny

***

Both women put sneakers on and Logan introduced Brooke to Cat's Ass.

Brooke was very impressed with the speed of the small sport bike as they took off down A1A South. She enjoyed the ocean view all the way to St. Augustine on the short half hour ride. Logan parked the bike across from the old Fort Matanzas entrance. She began telling Brooke the history of Florida's oldest city and the British battling the Spanish at the fort during the 1740s. They walked through the small shops admiring the different cultural artifacts. Brooke was a little pissed that she couldn't take anything back with them since they were on the bike. They drank a beer and ate a small snack at a tiny café along one of the streets before heading back to Jacksonville.

Later that evening, Logan made an extravagant candle light Italian dinner for the two of them, complete with a bottle of CA Montini Pinot Grigio. The bottle was finished before dinner was over. After dinner, Logan noticed Brooke was talking on her cell phone out on the balcony while she cleared the table. The woman returned after a brief conversation that Logan assumed had to do with FAA headquarters. These short discussions seemed to occur rather often. Logan was happy the NTSB didn't bother her constantly.

Logan poured herself a chilled glass of Navan before she stepped out onto the balcony next to Brooke, who was gazing at the stars and sipping her glass of wine.

"You never answered me last night." Brooke said quietly.

"What?" Logan looked quizzically at her.

77

"Why do you carry a gun on you? I noticed you didn't have it with you today. Do you only carry it at work?"

Logan's mind searched wildly. *Think of something Greer, think damn it think!...Just, be honest with the girl. It's not like she won't understand.*

"Well, it's sort of a long story."

Brooke turned towards Logan, but she didn't move, instead she leaned her stomach against the rail and starred into the ocean.

"If you don't..."

Logan cut her off. *It's now or never.*

"It was right after the 9/11 incident and I was going to one of my first accidents. I was a Safety Systems Specialist at the time and training to be an IIC. A 747 had crashed in the woods outside of Washington National. I remember it like it was yesterday." She took another sip of Navan, willing it to go down. "I was in D.C. about a mile from the crash site doing field training exercises. My ICC and I were on the scene just as fast as the rescue team. Part of the plane was in flames with passengers' still alive and trapped inside. Doing the only thing we knew to do, me, my Commander, and the paramedics tore through the wreckage and started pulling people out. I reached what was left of the front of the fuselage first and a man was stuck between the first class seat section and the cockpit. I could barely make out his features from all of the smoke. All I knew was he was alive and I was trying to save him. It wasn't until I pulled him loose that I noticed the gun in his hand. I turned my back to run and he shot me."

Brooke's eyes were about to pop out of her head. Logan took another slow swallow of the sweet burning liquid.

"That's the scar on your back?" Brooke asked. She remembered seeing the nasty scar up close while they were in the shower.

Logan nodded her head in admission.

"Apparently, the planes pilot had a .22 caliber pistol on him for safety because he was scared after 9/11. The man that shot me wrestled with the pilot and co-pilot to take over the plane just after take off. During the confrontation the pilots lost control of the plane and it went down in the woods. The pilots died on impact and he was pinned in the first class section by the cockpit entrance." Logan stopped again to take a long drink. Brooke just watched as the woman starred darkly at the ocean. "The bullet went into my back, fortunately missing most of the vital organs, and then it shattered a pair ribs when it went between them before getting stuck in my lung. I went down like a sack of potatoes when it hit me and luckily a policeman that was helping us remove people heard the shot. He saw the man trying to move despite having broken legs. The officer rushed to help him, before tripping over me, he saw a gun in the man's hand and shot him in the head. I was pulled from the plane and woke up in the ambulance. Luckily for me, the bullet barely penetrated the outer layer of my right lung. It took two hours worth of surgery to remove the metal fragment and repair the torn tissue. I tried to go back to work in less than a month when my ribs were healed. I had a full recovery, nothing to show except for a small inch wide scar on the right side of my lower back. I received a metal of bravery from the President, a key to the city from the Mayor, and various other awards from the NTSB. The only opposition that I had was my wanting to carry a firearm on me at all times will on the scene. I went through extensive training and I hold a few Small-Arms Certifications and Permits. Therefore, I can carry this gun on me anywhere and everywhere I go, basically, because I was shot in the line of duty."

Logan finished her glass of Navan and set it on the table next to the door. Brooke grabbed her hand and looked into dark blue eyes that were usually light green. Logan saw the couple of tears streaking down Brooke's face. She quickly grabbed the smaller woman and pulled her tightly into a loving embrace. This completely threw her off guard, she wasn't sure what to say or do so she just held her. Apparently, it upset Brooke to hear what happened to Logan.

A few minutes later Brooke broke the contact and apologized for getting so upset. She was surprised to see how hearing that story affected her so deeply.

"I'm so sorry you had to go through that. I'm also really sorry that I broke down in front of you like that." She had heard of the incident when she became an Investigator, but she never knew it was a woman or the name of the person for that matter.

"Hey, don't worry about it, I haven't told that story since it happened. I went to L.A. with Chaney to pursue her career. That lasted all of about three months, I wanted to go back, finish my training, and follow my own career. Chaney didn't try to stop me. She knew I would eventually go back. It's been over four years since the incident. I've tried to forget it, but I'm reminded of it every time I put that gun against my back. So, I live with it and move on. It's really not as bad as it seems…Come on." Logan grabbed Brooke's hand and walked inside towards the office.

They walked through the French doors, Logan turned the light on, and lead the way to the wall where the diploma's and degree's were alongside her Family Crest.

"These are my decorations, from my High School Diploma to my Master's in Aeronautical Science. Right here..." She pointed to the next set of frames. "I have all of my handgun certificates, and then over here are my honors from the incident."

Brooke looked closely at the military looking medal in the framed box and the golden key next to it. She noticed the other box frame that was full of military medals with a picture of a younger looking Logan and another picture of a young man that looked very similar to her.

"What are these?"

"Those on the top are my medals from Navy ROTC in high school, I was a Lieutenant. I joined the Navy, but my medical history with asthma kept me out of it. The other medals on the bottom, those were my Father's he was a Sergeant in the Marines, that's his picture on the bottom."

"Wow, that's really nice."

Logan was standing behind Brooke and she put her arms around the smaller woman and held her from behind.

"I bet you weren't expecting to find out all about me this weekend were you?"

"No, actually I wasn't. I have been curious though."

"It's ok. I'm not usually one to speak about myself. For some reason I let my guard down around you, plus you seem to ask the right questions."

Logan pulled Brooke against her and kissed her passionately, letting her lips linger imploringly.

"Besides that, you are a very hard woman to say no to Brooke McCabe." Logan smiled. Brooke noticed that Logan's eyes had returned to their naturally light Viridian Green color.

"Let's walk on the beach. It's a gorgeous night. Why should we let it go to waste?" Logan grinned cheerfully. Brooke agreed and the two women worked their way down through the Condo building until they were outside in the sand. They walked hand in hand for a few blocks and then turned around to head back. Brooke leaned closer and Logan stopped walking, stepped in front of Brooke, and wrapped her arms around her. The kiss started slow, but soon they were engulfed with desire, drinking from each other. Both women had their hands under the others clothes. Before they knew it, they were laying in the cold, sticky, wet sand rolling around barely dressed. Each woman hungry for the other as their bodies exploded together in the heated throws of passion.

An hour later, Logan and Brooke received some odd stares as they walked back into the Condo Lobby covered in sand from head to toe. They both just smiled and nodded their heads. As soon as the elevator door closed they were hysterical with laughter like two teenagers.

***

Monday morning arrived in its usual glory. Logan slapped the snooze button on the alarm, and then realized she was on the job still, so she immediately flew out of the bed like her ass was on fire. Into the bathroom and out of the closet, in twenty-five minutes she was walking out of the door. *I feel like I've been on a cloud all weekend.* She had taken Brooke back to the hotel Sunday evening and then fallen asleep. "Time to come back to reality Greer."

Logan finally found the break that she was looking for when the FDR film was fixed and she was able to read the data for the last ten minutes of the flight. The ATC tower claimed the pilot radioed that the fuel light for the left engine was flashing empty about two miles from JIA. The FDR and CVR both supported the ATC statements. The Pilot ordered the fuel lines to be opened up so that the right tank could feed the left engine. Soon after, the right fuel light began to flash and both engines shut off.

The Pilot then reported 'flame out' on both sides. He was ordered by the tower to open the flaps, pull the nose up, and glide the plane in. They came in too fast, over shot the runway by a few hundred yards and landed in the woods. The accident was blamed on faulty fuel lines that burst. This caused the leaking fuel to extinguish the engines instantly. The pilot was also at fault because he was instructed to pull up and open the flaps to slow the plane down as he glided in.

The FDR showed the flaps were opened sixty seconds before the landing, but the nose of the plane continued on a downward slope. This in turn would counteract against the drag on the fully open wing flaps, causing the planes decent speed to be much greater than suggested for an aircraft that size.

Logan spent the first half of her week buried in documents that had to be filled out and submitted to Washington for the finalization of the accident. It was

Thursday before Logan was alone with the sultry woman that had taken her body and mind prisoner over the last weekend.

"Hey Sherlock, I haven't seen you all week, I hear you solved this months mystery."

"Yeah, I'm sorry. I've been up to my asshole in papers trying to get to the damn facts. Do you remember last Thursday when we were discussing the possibility of a complete 'flame out'?"

"Yeah, ATC reported that to us."

"Yes well, the pilot should've had plenty of time to slow that plane for a safe landing; instead he overshot by three hundred yards."

"Right?"

"Come on Watson, work with me here." Logan grinned.

"The pilot was ordered flaps down and nose up to cut the decent speed. He only went with flaps. This only cut speed by a quarter at most."

"Damn, no wonder there was nothing left. They had to have been going double the normal landing speed."

"Exactly!"

"What about the fuel leak?"

"Your guys found some wiring problems and my guys found out that the fuel lines were too small causing the pressure to build up quicker. These fuel lines are made for a smaller aircraft. They couldn't take the degree of force that was being pushed through them and the left one burst first, then when they switched the fuel to both tanks it blew the other one almost in that instant. Of course the amount of fuel pouring out of the wings and into the turbines caused them to drown out."

"Damn…someone's ass in on the line here. I'm glad I don't handle Maintenance Logs or Regulations."

"You're telling me. Now I'll be in court for a month trying to sort this out for the legal department to take action against the Airline and the FAA."

"Ouch."

"Yeah."

"So I guess I better get to my pile of paperwork so I can head home. What a long couple of weeks." Brooke sighed.

"You know the worst part of it?"

"The Commercial Pilots Association?"

"Right, the CPA will make him look like the greatest pilot that ever flew a damn plane."

"Well, good luck with that." Brooke leaned forward and stole a quick kiss before going to her own assigned work area to finish her documentation.

Five

Logan worked day and night for the next six weeks trying vigorously to close the JAX case. She sat through weeks of trial and tribulation over who was to be held accountable for the catastrophe. Logan spent hours on the stand, sagaciously testifying the facts and her conclusion to the investigation.

In the end, the Maintenance Manager and Maintenance Supervisor were both fired, one for allowing the unapproved parts to be installed, the other for not logging any information on the aircraft parts change or update. Also, the Mechanic that performed the work was permitted to keep his position under an extreme probationary period, due to the fact that he was told by his immediate supervisor to install the improper equipment, when he refused stating the hoses were the wrong size, the manager then forced him to perform the job by threatening his employment in the airline industry.

On top of all of that, the FAA was once again slapped on the hand for not carrying out their duties, such as checking maintenance logs and routine mechanical inspections. Last but not least, the Airline received a large fine and since the deceased pilot and co-pilot were responsible for the safety of the aircraft while it was under their control, they were both considered liable for the accident.

***

Logan's cell phone rang on the kitchen counter. She stood up from the couch stretching her muscular form as she strolled across the room.

"Hey, Lynnie. What's up?"

"Not a whole hell of a lot. I just got back in town yesterday. How are you?"

"Tired, I've been busting my ass for months…"

"Yeah, I heard about the plane crash here, did you have to do anything with that?"

Hell I was in charge of it… "Yeah, I did some work with it at the airport."

"I'm glad we take a bus and not a plane, I'd be scared shitless to fly."

"Nah, it's not that bad, your odds of being on a doomed aircraft are almost nil."

"*Almost* being the keyword there my friend." Lynnie laughed and Logan joined her.

"I guess you're right, so what's going on tonight?"

"Not much…"

"You mean to tell me you just came home from your tour and the only thing you can think of doing is calling me at eight o'clock on a Friday night to discuss the odds of being in a plane crash?"

"No, I was hoping you'd get off your ass and join me for a drink to welcome me back to this shit hole."

"I see…hmm…meet me at the Martini Bar down by Joe's in a half hour."

"Sounds like a plan."

Logan arrived on time and parked Cats Ass by the front door. She saw Lynnie as she made her way to the bar. Logan bent down to hug the sitting woman who placed a small kiss on her check in return.

"Hey, babe." Lynnie always made it a point to show slight affection towards Logan. She knew nothing would come of it, so it quickly became a show of mere friendship. Logan sat on the stool next to Lynnie and ordered a cold beer.

"So, have you heard from our little friend lately?"

Logan looked puzzled. She quickly searched her brain for mutual contact between them. "Excuse me?"

"JT, has she called you or you called her?"

Still scanning the files in her head, Logan was waiting for the light bulb to go off.

"Who the hell is JT?"

"Oh I forgot you know her as Jensen…"

"Right…" *Duh Jensen Tirado, the mysterious EPA Scientist slash hot bar girl.*

"So…?"

"Uh…actually, I saw her while I was working with the plane that crashed."

"Huh…why would she be there?"

"She works for the EPA."

"Oh…what's with all of the acronyms?" Lynnie questioned.

"I don't know. Anyway she was there. We talked for a little while, but haven't spoken much since." Logan took a long swallow of her beer. Actually, they hadn't spoken at all since that day at the accident.

"I see. It sounds like she's playing you like she

88

does everyone else."

"I dunno, whatever I guess. So what's new with you?"

"The tour's halfway over, thank…" She looked down at the shot glass in front of her. "Patron'." She smiled.

Logan laughed and clinked her beer bottle against the shot glass that Lynnie was about to chug.

"Why don't you ever do shots with me? I ask you every time we're out together. I know you drink Cognac and other shit, but you wont do a shot you big puss."

"Touché." Logan smiled. "Usually, if I'm drinking shots then I'm on a mission to get slammed. You know that doesn't happen very often."

Lynnie giggled. "I think you're just a puss."

"Come on; let's play pool so I can kick your ass."

"Ha, you just might need a shot after I kick yours."

***

Logan slapped the snooze button on the noisy alarm clock and rolled back over, stretching her nude form across the king-sized bed. *Too tired…not yet…five more…*She was once again sound asleep. The black satin sheet contrasted with her naturally tanned skin. It rose and fell upon her chest, in sync with her breathing. She appeared angel-like as she slept peacefully, until the alarm sounded again.

"God damn it!" Logan flew out of the bed annoyed at the tiny machine that once again stole the serenity of her dream world.

Noon had come and gone by the time Logan cleared one pile of paperwork on her desk. She read document after document inside file after file until her normally light green eyes had turned to deep dark blue, simply out of frustration. Paperwork was quickly becoming her least favorite thing. Considering her desk was covered with it, she was starting to despise coming to work. A blue colored file full of official papers and a disc for her next assignment sat atop the huge pile. Logan opened the folder and checked her plane tickets before purposely sliding the classified file into her briefcase. *Three hours until departure.* She continued to slave away at the dockets on her desk.

When her cell vibrated against her belt she was reluctant to look down, but she smiled when she recognized the D.C. number.

"Hey, you."

"Hey, yourself." The familiar sweet voice spoke softly as Brooke smiled on the other end. "How's your day going?"

"Well, I'm up to my asshole in dockets. On top of that, I start my inspections today."

"Yuck. Hey are you coming my way at all?"

"Um...let me see..." Logan reached into her briefcase and opened the folder.

"Not really, BWI isn't too far from you I guess. I'm going there towards the end so probably about three weeks from now. This shit is always scattered around."

"I'm sorry Sweetie." Brooke's voice sounded seductive in its innocence.

"Hopefully I can spare enough time to at least

take you to dinner."

"That would be nice. I know how this business goes so I won't hold you to it if something comes up."

"That's nice of you."

"I'm not a bitch all the time." Brooke growled in a sexy low tone.

"True." Logan chuckled, thinking about the many times that the sexy woman had definitely been anything but a bitch.

***

The Gate Agents for the Airline called for the first class passengers. Logan was the first to board the 737 to Atlanta. Once the bird was in the air she opened her laptop and began going over the information on the disc. She was about to begin her second tour of inspection duty. The first tour was abruptly interrupted. She hoped this one would go by smoothly. She always spent time in December and January and then again in June and July going over the nations most popular airports with a fine tooth comb. Every year the sequence was rearranged into two sets of twenty-five, she never knew which cities she would be visiting until the confidential envelope arrived.

***

A little over an hour later Logan was speaking to the CSI of the Airport, he took her on a tour of the facility making sure to stop and speak to every Airline Manager as well as checking all of the Airline Maintenance Logs. A few hours later she was back on a plane, this time heading for Milwaukee.

Logan spent another two and a half weeks going through Chicago, Memphis, Miami, Newark, and Kansas City. She had only found a few minor mistakes consisting of improper paperwork handling and missing aircraft inspection sheets in some of the logs. Logan was in a better mood this time around the tour and found herself only reprimanding three people. Three people that she would've normally fired without a care in the world.

Now, taxiing down the runway in New Orleans where she had observed first hand, the devastation Hurricane Katrina left behind almost a year ago. The exhausted blond was finally on her way to Baltimore, hoping to have a nice quiet evening alone with Brooke before starting the last three weeks of her inspection tour. She closed her eyes, desperately trying to rest on the plane. Twenty minutes later she awoke to smashing her head on the window sill. They were flying through some turbulence inside a small storm over Illinois.

"Ouch!"

The first class flight attendant saw the whole episode take place from her jump seat next to the cockpit door. She winced and gave Logan a heartfelt crooked smile, as in saying she was sorry. When the seatbelt sign went off the small brunette walked quickly to Logan.

"I'm so sorry Agent, is your head okay?"

Logan was supposed to be incognito when she flew Domestic Carriers, appearing as a business woman. Although her name and position were on the passenger manifest, none of the flight crew ever referred to her as anything but a regular passenger, until now. Logan believed it was because knowing who she was made them nervous.

Logan smiled at the petite woman.

"It hurts but I'm fine."

"I didn't realize you were asleep until I was already strapped in. Otherwise, I would've woken you up. I really am sorry."

"Don't be, I promise I wont die from smacking my head on an airplane window."

"I hope not, that would on my conscience forever."

Both women laughed. Then, she went back to her job of checking on the passengers. A short time later the plane landed safely. Logan called Brooke to let her know that she had arrived and was on the way to her room at the Hilton.

***

Logan looked through the small peep hole before answering the soft knock at the door. She smiled at the deformed figure standing on the other side of the door. *She's so damn sexy!* Brooke walked in dressed in gray pants and a wine colored blouse. Her heels made her stand slightly taller than Logan who was now barefooted.

"Hey, sexy." Brooke stepped forward and threw her arms around Logan's neck as she pressed her lips to Logan's. The sensual kiss lingered slowly as both women enjoyed the heat that passed between them.

Logan looked into soft green eyes. She tenderly held the woman in front of her, willing herself to let go so she could welcome her guest inside.

"Hey, yourself." Logan took Brookes hand and led her into the large hotel suite.

"Looks like you're getting the Presidential

treatment."

"For the most part, although, I have had my share of rundown ratty looking rooms." Logan winced, thinking about the rooms she was forced to stay in when she volunteered to join the International Airport Tour. *Yuck!*

Brooke watched Logan's facial expressions and knew she was lost in thought.

"Hey, whatcha thinking about Sherlock?"

"Uh…nothing,…just a trip to Europe that I'd like to forget. So, are you hungry?"

"For you!" Brooke stepped out of her heels, making her eye level with Logan's mouth. She slowly pushed the taller woman back onto the large bed. Logan held onto Brooke and pulled the sneaky woman down on top of her as she fell back. They rolled around on the bed kissing and tasting each other. Seconds later, their clothes were frantically removed and tossed onto the floor at the foot of the bed.

"I've missed you so much," Brooke whispered into a soft earlobe.

"I've missed you too," Logan mumbled into Brooke's hair that had come undone and fell loosely down her back.

Logan felt Brooke's wetness against her thigh as the small woman laid on top of her. She looked passionately into beautiful hazel-green eyes, and ran her hands down silky smooth, olive-colored skin. Logan's hand went no further than the honey-colored curls between Brooke's legs She began massaging the swollen mound of nerves. Brooke slowly moved back and forth. Logan could sense the other woman's body wanting more. She easily slid two fingers inside of the woman on top of her, penetrating as deep as she could before completely removing them and then starting over again until Brooke took control and began sliding herself down to Logan's palm and back up again, thrusting her hips harder and faster.

"Ah...Ah..." She cried out as the orgasm overtook her body with raw desire.

Logan withdrew from her slowly, feeling the tense muscles wrapped around her fingers. Brooke's limp body collapsed against the warm frame underneath her as Logan wrapped her arms around the fascinating woman and held her close.

They remained in their chosen position for a few long minutes. Neither woman spoke of the passion that passed between them. Brooke severed the contact first, rolling onto the bed next to Logan.

"I do believe it's your turn." She growled with a wink as she slid down the bed, stopping when she was eye level with Logan's center.

"And what is it that you have in mind, Miss McCabe?" Logan teased back.

"Lay back and relax, you'll soon find out." Brooke positioned herself between Logan's legs and began running her tongue up and down softly teasing throbbing layers of skin beneath the blond curls.

"Ah!" Logan reached down for Brooke's hand and the woman quickly pulled away from the moist center.

"Huh uh...nope...no hands, Agent Greer, not this time."

"But..." Logan pleaded, longing for the other woman's touch.

"No hands..." Brooke flashed a wolfish grin

95

before running her tongue seductively across the same sensitive path.

Logan's body jerked from the delicate touch. She contemplated reaching for the sly woman again, but decided against it, begging her not to stop the orgasm she was leisurely inducing.

"Ah…" She was fighting against herself not to put her hands on the woman between her legs. "Brooke…please let…I need to hold you…" The climax passed through Logan like a runaway freight train. She sat straight up in the bed, grabbed Brooke and pulled the small woman up into her arms. Their lips met for the most intense kiss that either woman had ever felt. Logan was sure her heart was speaking of words that her mind wasn't ready to acknowledge.

***

Logan awoke to her cell phone ringing obnoxiously. She rolled over to answer it. "Greer." She said sharply, realizing she was alone in the room.

The conversation with the NTSB-Major Aircraft Accident Office was ending when she heard the hotel room door click open. *Uh, Hello?* Her eyes searched the room for her Sig-Sauer. She had completely forgotten about putting it in her briefcase the night before. Logan decided to sneak up on her unexpected guest. She stood against the wall leading to the living room.

Brooke, carrying a handful of breakfast items for her sleeping lover, walked nonchalantly across the living area and through the bedroom doorway.

Logan's naked body dove onto her from the side, sending the small woman and the food crashing to the floor with Logan ending on top of the pile.

"God damn it Logan! Ouch!" Brooke muttered with her face smashed into the carpet.

"You scared the shit out of me!" Logan stood up and winced when she saw the small woman flattened and covered in food.

"What the fuck did you tackle me for?" Brooke pushed herself up off of the floor, wiping the juice, bacon, muffins, and toast from her recently dry-cleaned clothing.

Logan grinned sheepishly. "Uh…I'm sorry?" She flashed her best please forgive me green eyes.

"My god woman, you are by far the most skittish person I have ever met." Brooke shook her head and laughed at the mess on the floor.

"What is that?" Logan stared at the mess.

"It *was* your breakfast in bed. I went down to the continental breakfast looking for coffee and I decided to surprise you."

Logan chuckled loudly. "I'm so sorry, sweetheart."

"Yeah well, can't say I didn't try." She smiled.

"We should probably get you out of those dirty clothes so they can be cleaned."

"Oh really, and what do you suppose we do while the hotel staff cleans my now edible business suit?"

"I do believe I could come up with something." Logan spoke back in an egotistical Scottish accent, and mocking the English figure Sherlock Holmes.

***

Later that Morning, Logan was flipping through

the file of FAA recommendations for Baltimore-Washington International Airport, preparing for her brief meetings with each of the Air Carrier Managers. The first leg of this tour went better than expected, partly because of the mood that Brooke always seemed to put her in. She hoped the second leg faired the same. A faint smile crossed her face when her thoughts formed a rather naked picture of the woman on her mind. *Get with it Greer. You have work to do. Daydreaming is the last thing you need to be doing.*

***

Her first of nineteen meetings was with the Delta Airlines Manager. They were starting to pick back up after filing Chapter Eleven last year with a few other major air carriers. Logan followed her normal routine of going through their Aircraft Maintenance Logs with a fine toothed comb, observing the ground crew on an in coming or out going flight, then counseling the Manager on any mistakes that she found. Five hours later, Logan was preparing to board her next flight. This, time she was on her way to Denver, Newport News, and then Boston's Logan International to finish out her week.

***

Logan tried desperately to sleep on the plane. Her eyes drifted to an image of the beautiful woman that took her completely by surprise and made her feel human again. *What the hell is wrong with me?*

"Would you like a drink Ma'am?" The petite Flight Attendant with blonde hair spoke softly.

Fate Vs. Destiny

Logan's eyes flew open to see the face belonging to the voice in front of her.

"I'm sorry I didn't notice you were sleeping. Would you like a beverage?"

"Uh...no I'm fine, thank you."

"Yes you are," The Beach Barbie look alike spoke just loud enough for Logan to hear her. She smiled and continued to serve the rest of the first class passengers.

My god, what is with women these days? A year ago you couldn't pay for a lousy date, now they're falling in your lap. There has got to be something in the air. Logan shook her head and yawned as she closed her eyes once again.

***

Logan finally ran into the snag that she had been anticipating in Houston at the George Bush Intercontinental Airport. Two of the twenty-three Airlines were missing important documents regarding recent incidents, four of them had FAA recommendations that were never put into action, and five of them didn't have an Airline Manager on Duty. The usually composed bombshell was furious. She unbuttoned her black pants-suit jacket, followed the Airport Director and the CSI into the Directors office and slammed the door shut.

"Mr. Baxter, you have no idea what is going on in this facility. I am completely appalled. I don't even know where to begin."

"I take full responsibility for the confusion and chaos that you have encountered today, Agent Greer. I'm very sorry."

Logan turned towards the balding man dressed in

a dark blue business suit. At first glance he appeared much older than he actually was.

"Thank you, but no thank you, Chief Hartlin. This is one of the worst Airports that I have ever seen throughout my history of doing these inspections. If it were up to me, I would've shut this place down five hours ago. I mean one or two mistakes I can handle, we're all human. But, eleven out of twenty-three airlines had a major violation. I hope you guys realize you have just set me back at least a week, probably two. Now I have to sit here and baby-sit you both while you fix at least twenty-five percent of these problems, I can't have clearance to fly out of here until I can send at least a score of seventy-five percent to Washington. Trust me those guys don't play; even with a rating of seventy-five percent you would both be unemployed. Now, I need to call them and tell them that you managed a total score of forty-nine percent."

Logan was trying not to yell too loud since the walls were thin in the office area, but her pissed-off meter was nearing the high mark. The director finally opened his fat mouth, with a southern draw he spoke evenly.

"Agent Greer, I'm not asking you to do anything other than your job here at George Bush, but I am asking you to at least give me a chance to straighten this mess out."

"You lost your chances the day you decided to stop doing your job around here. Thousands of peoples lives are under your control everyday and you sit in the middle of these four walls doing god knows what while you let the cast of Hee Haw run this damn airport! The only thing I can say, Mr. Baxter, is you better have a complete management staff here within the hour or you

100

will be in the unemployment line before the sun comes up. As for you Chief Hartlin, you have twenty-four hours to find the missing documents for both of those incidents and you need to have at least two of those recommendations completed. I could care less about saving your jobs. But, I would really like to fly out of here sometime this month. Oh, and by the way, you can expect the FAA here in the morning as well." She slammed the door again as she exited the room. *Idiots, god damn idiots!*

"Mr. Hudson?"

"Yes."

"This is Agent Logan Greer. I'm in the field on the second leg of the ASI tour."

"Yes Greer, I know. What's wrong?"

"I'm at GBI in Houston, we have a serious problem. They have a total score of forty-nine percent."

"Excuse me? What the hell. How did this happen?"

"Well Sir, they are missing some incident documents, FAA Recs, and five of the airlines didn't have a MOD."

"This is a code red, Agent. Follow protocol, they have twenty-four hours to hit the seventy-five percent mark or we will shut-down the facility."

"Yes Sir, I know. I gave the Director and the CSI specific instruction. I will be here in the morning to meet with the FAA Inspectors. I will have to come back here in two weeks to inspect again, so my schedule will be off slightly."

"That's not a problem. Our main priority is Houston right now. Keep me informed, Agent Greer."

Graysen Morgen

***

When she finally made it back to her hotel, she hit the bar running. Logan closed her eyes tightly, trying not to anticipate the next week of paperwork and meetings that would capture her every waking moment. *Just this once, please let this go smoothly. I'm tired and ready to go home to my peaceful serenity and salt air. I'm going to sleep for days. Ha...who am I kidding?. I'll have four hours of sleep max and then it's back to square one.* Logan downed the chilled glass of Navan in front of her and ordered another round.

Six

Logan was already awake and packing for her long awaited flight out of Houston, when the cell phone on the night stand echoed across the hotel room as it rang the familiar Waltz tune.

"Greer."

"Agent Greer, this is Walter Hudson with the NTSB."

Logan felt her chest and shoulders tighten. *This can't be good, so much for home sweet home.*

"Yes, Sir?"

"We just received a report that Air Force One has crash landed at Randolph Air Force Base outside of San Antonio. I have arranged a rental car for you at George Bush International Airport. The next flight going that way doesn't leave for three hours and you can drive there in two or two and a half. Your team is about to leave now on a private jet with Homeland Security and the FAA."

"Was the President on board?"

"The only information I know at this time is that it was Flight AF1 215. That's Air Force One plane number two, which is a seven forty seven. Greer, the Marines and the Press will be all over this, you're the most qualified Investigator In Charge for this accident. Don't let them push you around out there."

103

"You don't have to worry about that Sir, I can hold my own."

"I know you can. Good luck and keep me informed."

Logan closed her phone and looked in the mirror at her ghost white face. "Son of a bitch!" She ran her hand through her hair and let out the breath she had been holding since she heard the words Air Force One. *Get it together girl!*

***

The black Ford Explorer SUV stopped abruptly at the entrance gate to Randolph Air Force Base. Logan handed her badge through the window to the Air Force Captain standing at the gate next to the Marine Staff Sergeant MP holding the rifle. She removed her sun glasses and gave the man her best "eat shit" grin. He immediately gave her directions to the runway and waved her forward.

Logan saw nothing but flashing lights and at least a hundred G.I. Joe's with AK-47 and M-16 rifles surrounding the plane. She slowed the SUV to a stop next to an MP Jeep parked a hundred yards away. She stepped out with her badge folded open and hanging from the left front pocket of her black suit jacket. Logan was immediately bombarded from every direction.

"Holy shit!"

"This is a highly Classified Government Area. You do not have permission to be on this end of the base. Get back in your vehicle, Ma'am, and leave at once, forget everything you have seen here." The Marine, standing mere inches from her face, was screaming.

"Obviously you overlooked the badge in front of your face." She reached up and pressed her badge towards his face. "I'll let it slide this time. I suggest you not let this happen again."

"Who the hell are you? You still can't be here, lady. I will put you back in your vehicle if I have to."

God damn idiot! "My name is Agent Logan Greer, I'm an Investigator for the NTSB. That would mean the Government has sent me here. I suggest you step aside before I have you removed from this base for interfering with an Official Investigation." She smiled with sarcasm as the young grunt stepped aside to let her pass by him. As she made her way towards the large jumbo jet she noticed that only the under side was damaged and the plane appeared to be sitting on its belly with no landing gears at all. There were gouge marks all the way down the asphalt runway where the plane had begun its landing.

"Who was on board? Has anyone touched anything? Were there any witnesses on the ground?" She asked the man that appeared to be in charge of the soldiers.

"You must be from D.C."

"Did the badge give it away or my sense of urgency?" She asked sarcastically.

"The black suit, and the shiny badge."

"Well?"

"Well what?"

Stupid fucking jar-head! "Who was on the plane? Did anyone see it land?"

"Yeah, the two pilots were on there with three crew members. The control tower saw it land and a few mechanics were on the ground."

"Okay, that's a start."

Logan was beside herself trying to deal with the useless half-wits in front of her. She walked around the inside of the plane and then the outside taking notes. Matthew Taglia with Homeland Security arrived along with Brooke McCabe and the FAA group. The NTSB team was just ahead of them as they made their way towards the plane.

"Good to see you again Agent Greer."

"Hello, Mr. Taglia, Miss McCabe, it's nice to see you again."

"Likewise, Agent Greer." Brooke smiled openly and Logan returned with a grin.

Matthew began to secure the sight with the Marines. Logan stepped away to address the two investigation units.

"Alright listen up everyone, here is the situation. The President was not on board, only the Pilot, co-pilot, and three crew members. No fatalities, only minor cuts and bruises. The control tower was in clear view of the landing, a few ground crewmembers were the first on the scene."

She pointed to a few of the FAA Team Members and then a few of her own team members. "You guys get statements from the tower and the ground. Our main priority is the Black Box and the CVR. From the looks of it, I would say we have a mechanical failure here, but I can't be certain. Miss McCabe, I need you to get a hold of the maintenance log, contact the last air station to perform any work on the aircraft, also contact the departing air field. We need statements from the ground crew and the tower there as well. I believe that's all for now. You should all have my cell number, call me with any information or questions." Logan began to walk away.

"Where are you going?" Logan turned towards the familiar sweet voice. Brooke was standing there in a dark gray pants suit and a white blouse. Her long hair was pulled up in a bun behind her head.

"I'm going to the infirmary to get the statements from the pilots and crew."

"I really meant what I said. It's good to see you again. I've missed you." Brooke smiled.

"It's nice to see you too. What's with the pants?"

"I was already wearing this when I got the call. I would rather be in a skirt."

"Yeah, I was looking forward to that." Both women laughed and Logan smiled seductively.

***

Two days later Logan was in her hotel room listening to the CVR for the hundredth time and reading statement after statement until she was blue in the face. *You need a break, Greer.* She called Brooke's cell number.

"Hello?"

"Hey you, wanna meet me? I'm starving and in need of a drink."

"I can't. I'm sorry."

"Okay." Logan could swear she heard a man's voice in the background.

"Where are you?"

"My room. Watching TV and doing paperwork."

"Have a good night then." She hung up and laid her head back against the pillows.

***

The first week of the investigation had ended and Logan was sure she had the cause of the accident pinpointed to a landing gear failure. She called Brooke into the small Base office that she was working out of.

"Let me run this by you. I may have something here."

The beautiful, usually seductive woman was hesitant and guarded every time she was around Logan. Logan was still trying to figure out what was bothering her companion.

"What if the landing gears never deployed?"

"What do you mean?"

"The plane landed on its belly, the landing gears were never down, none of them."

"Logan that's absurd, all of the lights were lit up, there were no warnings."

"I know it doesn't sound right, just think about it for a second. What if the computer thought the wheels were lowered, but they weren't? The co-pilot said he heard a siren as the plane hit the ground. I'm telling you, that was the warning and the computer didn't register until after it hit and then sounded the siren. Plus, the landing gears are all still intact."

"It doesn't make sense. The light was lit up showing all of the gears were down."

"I ran it on my laptop in the simulator and the accident was almost identical."

"It can't be."

"Brooke, I need you to agree with me on this."

"Show me the model on the computer." Brooke

108

stepped around the desk and stood behind Logan. The scent of her lover was driving her crazy with desire. She forced her hands by her side to keep from touching the woman that was mere inches away from her. The computer simulated the scenario that Logan had programmed. Brooke watched in amazement.

"Oh my god Logan, you're right. How the hell..." Logan turned around and pressed her lips against the softest mouth she had ever felt. Brooke gave in and opened her lips slightly to feel Logan's tongue massage her own. Logan grabbed Brooke's waist and pulled her down into her lap. Both women kissed and pawed at each other.

"I miss you so much." Brooke whispered into Logan's ear as she bit it softly.

"God I miss you too!"

A knock on the door broke their contact abruptly.

"Agent Greer, I finished those reports that you wanted." A young NTSB Team member stood in the doorway.

"Thanks."

Brooke followed the young man out of the office without a look back towards the desk. Logan wasn't sure what that was about, but figured she'd find out later. She was use to Brooke's mysteriousness.

***

A few days later, Logan presented her office with her conclusion and was preparing to go live on TV to tell the public what caused the Air Force One plane to crash land. *Come on, Greer, this isn't as bad as you think it is. It's a camera and a bunch of reporters. You deal with them all the time.* She ran a nervous hand through her short blond hair and straightened the baby blue collar on the blouse she was wearing under her black pants suit. Her badge was folded and hanging out of the left breast pocket of her jacket.

"Agent Greer, are you ready?"

"As ready as I'll ever be." A woman opened the office door and escorted Logan down the hall to a large conference room that held the press and their infamous cameras. The Governor of Texas was standing at the podium and had already begun his opening statements.

"Now I'll turn the mike over to National Transportation Safety Board Investigator In Charge Agent Logan Greer."

Logan stepped up next to him and shook his hand as he walked away.

"Good Morning Ladies and Gentlemen, let me begin by saying we at the NTSB are very pleased to have concluded this investigation in a timely manner and believe the results are unquestionable. The cause of the Air Force One accident was due to a chain of events. I'm going to give you a brief overview and then take your questions. First, the pilot and co-pilot prepared the plane for landing as they have over a hundred times. The pilot pulled the landing gear lever and the green light lit up. Both the pilot and co-pilot proceeded with the landing as they normally would. When they were approximately inches from touch down, the warning siren sounded and they began to land. The wheels never lowered and this caused the plane to land on its belly and skid roughly a thousand feet before coming to a stop. As you know, there was only a small crew on the plane. They all survived with minor cuts and bruises."

"Agent Greer, Frank Jones with CNN News. Were there any warning lights or anything to let the pilots know the wheels weren't down?"

"No, unfortunately the computer failed to pick up the signal from the wheels, meaning the on board computer was functioning as if the wheels had in fact deployed. There is a red light that flashes in the cockpit and a warning siren. In this case the computer sent the warning too late for the pilots to react."

Logan spent another twenty minutes answering the questions from the press and then left the podium. She stopped at the office down the hall to speak with her team and the FAA. Since the investigation was now closed she needed to dismiss everyone. As the door opened to the small square room Logan's eyes caught a glimpse of an image that she could never have imagined. Brooke McCabe was in Matthew Taglia's arms with her lips pressed against his. The rest of the FAA team was caught in conversation with the NTSB representatives and a few Homeland Security Officers. Logan stepped back, trying desperately to get a hold of herself. Her blood was boiling with anger and jealousy in a mix of mass confusion.

"Hey, Agent Greer, nice speech." Matthew broke contact with Brooke long enough to shake Logan's hand as she walked past them. She politely returned the handshake and gave a slight nod of her head, refusing to look at Brooke. She stopped in the center of the room to gather everyone's attention.

"The investigation of Flight AF1 215 is officially closed. You are all hereby dismissed and may leave for your departing flights as soon as you are able. I thank you all for your cooperation and assistance these past few weeks." With another quick nod of her head she started for the door. Brooke quickly followed her out of the room.

"Slow down, I need to talk to you."

"No you don't, there's nothing we need to say to each other."

Logan turned down the exit corridor that led to the open lot where her rental SUV was parked. Brooke was right on her heels as the door to the outside swung open. Logan continued walking straight ahead.

"Listen to me please! I need to explain this to you."

Logan clinched her hands as tight as they would go. Her knuckles were as white as her face as she turned around.

"I don't ever want to see your face or hear your name again as long as I live. If I was dead that would be too soon."

"Damn it we work together so you'll have to see me and that was really hateful Logan. Don't talk to me like that!" Brooke was mad at Logan for not talking to her and sad at the same time for making Logan hurt so badly.

"Fuck you, Brooke, or should I say fuck him since I'm sure you are. Boy was I a sucker. Tell me was it funny to sneak away with me behind his back?"

"No Logan please, it wasn't like that."

"Okay were you fucking him behind my back then?"

"Me and you were never serious. We never said we wouldn't see other people."

"I get it. I didn't exactly not see other people, but I didn't start relationships or fuck them, especially after I let you into my life by bringing you to my house and into my god damn bed!"

"Shut up and let me explain this to you please!" Brooke spat out.

"Go back inside to your little boyfriend Brooke. We're through here."

"Logan he's asked me to marry him. I'm sorry. I wanted to tell you, but there was never a good time."

"Wow, you bitch! You have some fucking nerve! Get away from me. I'm serious Brooke I never want to see you again." Logan's blood was boiling. She wanted to knock Brooke's head off of her shoulders.

"I'm sorry Logan."

"Fuck you!" Logan opened to the door to the SUV, climbed in and slammed the door shut. The tires squealed as she sped off. Brooke could do nothing but stand there and watch her leave.

Seven

Logan couldn't feel the heat burning in her chest. She was past the point of raging anger. Her mind raced wildly with images of the past year. Her arms worked in rhythm as she pounded the heavy weight bag uncontrollably. *Left...right...left, right...How could she do this to me? Left...right, right...left...What a fucking bitch! I thought she was so much more. Right...left...left, right...I let her run right fucking over me. Right...left...right, right...left, left, right...Damn you, Brooke.*

She was oblivious to the sweaty tears flowing down her cheeks and the blood trickling from her knuckles. As she backed away from the black leather enemy hanging in front of her, her knees buckled and Logan's body hit the floor with a loud thud.

***

Logan woke up in a puddle of sweaty tears tainted with blood on the hardwood floor of the gym. She glanced around happy to see that she was still alone. *I must have fainted...holy shit!* She shook her head and wiped her eyes with her towel as she stood up. The stinging pain in her upper body was now apparent. She made her way back to her condo and stopped directly in front of the liquor cabinet in the kitchen.

Three and a half chilled and filled to the top glasses of Navan later she was passed out on the couch. She woke up a few hours later and started all over again, polishing off her second bottle in a few days. In less than a week she had become a walking, talking zombie, relying on alcohol and a steady drunk feeling to keep her going.

Logan barely crawled through the next few weeks. After a late Friday night meeting she sped home, stripped her clothes, sunk down into the steaming whirlpool tub, and laid her head back against a towel on the side. *What the hell is happening to me? I'm so much stronger than this. Logan you need to pick yourself up girl. This isn't like you. You knew it wouldn't last. My god! What the hell would I do if I got a call right now to go to a crash? What then? Wake the fuck up! I have to get you out of my mind. Whatever it takes.*

Logan shot up out of the tub and ran into the closet only half dried off. She came back out in jeans, a slim fitting long sleeve baby blue colored t-shirt, and brown Doc Marten shoes. Her hair was still a mess when she walked out of her Beach Palace. Logan moved towards her garage. After a few quick movements, she was ready to take Cats Ass out on the town. The motorcycle howled as she sped off towards her destination, 'Jane's Place', the infamous lesbian local watering hole.

Logan went straight to the bar and ordered a beer. Before the cold beer could make its way down her throat, a warm body was against her back, a soft scent lingering in the air around her. She could feel the warm breath on her neck as the stranger spoke.

"I've missed you."

Logan turned towards the familiar smell and wrapped her arms around Jensen.

"Hey, you."

Their lips met as they kissed passionately. Logan could feel Jensen's hands against her bare back as the petite blond slid her hands under the shirt. The kiss lasted longer than anticipated. Both women pulled away slightly out of breath, neither of them noticing the stares coming from around the room. Half of the room wanted to be in Jensen's shoes and the other half in Logan's.

"I saw you on TV. You're so different when you're working."

"Like you have room to talk, you caught me completely off guard."

Jensen smiled. "You never called."

Logan looked down into intense gray eyes. "You stopped text messaging."

"Yeah, I've been really busy with work."

"You can say that three times over."

Both women stepped away from each other and drank their beers. Jensen walked back over to her friends and Logan turned back towards the bar where the bar manager was waiting for her.

"Hey, famous high powered government agent hottie!"

"Logan started laughing. "What?"

"I saw your cute little ass on TV. I would've never imagined you as a government asshole."

"Bridgette, you have no idea."

Both women laughed as the bartender slid another beer in front of Logan.

"This one's on me."

"Thanks."

"So are you on that sexy machine of yours tonight?"

"As always."

"When are you gonna take me for a ride?"

"When your girlfriend stops threatening to beat my ass."

"Not likely, especially since the whole bar knows who you are now. We had the news on the night they aired you in your power suit telling the whole world what caused that plane crash."

"That's lovely."

"Honey if these girls don't want to fuck you, they damn sure wanna be you."

"HAHA Oh my god! That's all I need."

"Seriously, why didn't you ever tell anyone what you did? Since you were the topic of conversation for the rest of that night, it seems that no one in here knew what you did for a living. Except JT, she said that she's seen you on the job."

"Yeah, we had to work together not long ago."

"So I heard. I figured you were a scientist nerd like her. Boy was I way off."

"Nah, not too far. She works on soil and I work on crashed aircraft."

Bridgette smiled and shook her head.

Logan took out her cell phone and sent *Wanna get out of here?* to Jensen in a text.

She kept her back to the woman and conversation with the bartender and a few other people sitting at the bar. Her phone vibrated and she read the text that was sent back to her…*Where did you have in mind?*

Graysen Morgen

Logan text back...*Anywhere you wanna go, as long as we are alone.*

Jensen sent... *Follow me out.*

Logan watched Jensen make her way towards the door.

"That's my cue guys, talk to you next time." Logan stood up and followed the blonde out of the bar. Logan got on the bike and Jensen got into a black SUV. Logan followed Jensen to an apartment complex on Southside Boulevard. The black SUV stopped in a parking spot in the back and Jensen hopped out. Neither woman spoke as Logan walked behind her up the stairs and into the apartment. Jensen gave Logan a quick tour of her place, leaving the bedroom for last.

Within minutes both woman were up against the wall, their lips pressed tightly together, and their tongues fighting for control. Jensen quickly had Logan's shirt half way off, her jeans unbuttoned, and her hand massaging the wet mound of nerves. Logan had enough of letting someone else have all of the control. She picked Jensen up and laid her back onto the bed and straddled on top of her. She pulled her upper body up off of the bed and stripped off Jensen's shirt and bra together. Logan unbuttoned Jensen's jeans, leaned down and slowly ran her tongue from Jensen's panties, around her pierced belly button, all the way up her muscular stomach and between her breasts. She stopped her tongue when she found Jensen's left ear and bit down.

"Ah goddamn you're so sexy." Jensen moaned with pleasure.

"Honey, you haven't seen anything yet." Logan growled back as she slipped Jensen's jeans off, tossed them across the room and finished with her hand sliding right under Jensen's panties and into the wet folds.

"Ah...like that...yeah!" Jensen said breathlessly.

Two minutes later Jensen had a hand full of Logan's short blond hair, tugging and forcing Logan to go deeper inside of her. She shuttered and collapsed in Logan's arms as the orgasm took over her body.

Logan quickly fixed her clothes and promised the night to be continued as she rushed out the door. The bike sped through the dark quiet streets of Jacksonville, as tears streamed down her face. She was furious with herself for what she had just done and beating herself up for not staying the night. "Damn you Brooke, damn you for what you have done to me!"

After she parked the bike and closed the garage, she went through the gate to the ocean and plopped down in the sand. The tears were still flowing steadily. *What the fuck is wrong with me? I'm sitting here balling my eyes out and I don't know if it's because I feel as if I cheated on someone or because I ran out on a beautiful girl lying naked in my arms wanting more.* She remained in that same spot for an hour beating herself up mentally. Finally, Logan stood up and made her way inside and up the elevator to her penthouse condo.

***

A week later Logan had just finished a crazy, paperwork filled day in her office at JIA. She thought about Jensen as she drove passed the bar on her way home. Feeling like a total asshole, she picked up her cell phone and scrolled through the phonebook. It rang only once.

"Hello?"

119

"Jensen?"

"Yeah?"

"Hey it's uh…Logan."

"Hey what's up?"

"I'm on my way home, listen…uh…I …" She took a deep breath. "I wanted to apologize for the other night. I didn't…"

"Why? There's nothing to be sorry for. I had a nice time."

"I did too, but I'm sorry I sort of ran out on you. I…"

"Hey, don't let it bother you, it's not like we're in love or dating. I totally understand. Hell it's not like I've never done that. I do wish I would've had a chance to take care of you though."

Logan was lost for words. She wasn't use to apologizing for being a player. Normally she wouldn't even call the person.

"What are you doing tonight?"

"I dunno, are you going out?"

"I'd like to take you to dinner."

"That could possibly be arranged. I just got home not long ago so I need to shower."

"Yeah, I'm still on my way home."

"I don't even know where you live."

"I live at the beach, but I'll pick you up. We can go somewhere in your area if you want."

"I don't care. Call me when you're on the way."

"Sure thing." Logan hung up the phone, surprised that Jensen hadn't made her feel like a first class piece of shit.

She rushed around showering, picked out a pair of jeans, a canary yellow polo shirt, and brown flip flops.

Her green eyes glowed almost iridescent next to her bright blond hair.

***

Their dinner went by quick and both women made it a point to see each other again. Logan got out of the truck and walked Jensen to the door. She leaned in to kiss her cheek and Jensen pushed her back against the door, pressed their lips together and let her tongue do the talking.

A half hour later both women were on the living room floor covered in sweat with a pile of clothes next to them. The sudden sound of footsteps got their attention real quick as Jensen shot up off of the floor.

"My roommate's home!"

"Son of a bitch!"

They both grabbed their clothes and bolted towards Jensen's bedroom. A bare ass was seen as Bridgette, the bartender slash roommate, walked through the front door. She was laughing hysterically.

"Caught ya JT!" Bridgette yelled.

"Fuck, this is all I need." Logan grimaced out as she hastily threw her clothes back on.

"It's not the end of the world. She saw you leave with me last week, she's not stupid."

"Yeah, well it wasn't as obvious then." Logan shook her head, half pissed that she'd been caught, and slightly laughing at the situation at the same time.

"Don't you make enough money to live alone? Who the hell has a roommate at your…wait a second how old are you again?"

Jensen giggled. "I've already told you, besides,

I'm old enough to have a college degree, and yes…live on my own. It's complicated."

"You and she aren't…I mean she has a girlfriend. I saw them together."

"No me and Bridgette are not together, no way."

"Whew, okay so I guess that's my cue to butt out huh."

"Yeah."

Both women walked out of the room, their clothes were slightly disheveled. Jensen had put her hair up and Logan's hair didn't look much different since always wore it messy looking.

"Well hello their ladies!" Bridgette shot an ear to ear grin from her position on the couch. "It's nice to see you again, Logan."

"Yes, as always Bridgette. What's up?"

"Not a whole hell of a lot. It seems I missed the party."

"Yup. So, Jensen I need to get going. I have an early meeting in the morning."

"I'll walk you out."

Eight

Two weeks later Logan was laying on the couch watching TV when her cell phone started it's Addam's Family Waltz.

"Greer."

"Hey, what's up?" The scratchy voice on the other end spoke.

"Lynnie, how the hell are you stranger?"

"Good, I just back from visiting my family in Georgia."

"That's good."

"Yeah, so I hear you're fucking JT."

"What, holy shit!!" Logan almost fell off of the couch.

Lynnie laughed. "Did you think I wouldn't find out? Hell the whole bar probably knows."

"That's just fucking great."

"It is isn't it." Lynnie laughed.

"What?"

"It's fucking great or at least it has to be. Everyone at the bar wants you both."

"Whatever. How did you find out?"

"I have my ways."

"Great, Lynnie the super spy. Haha."

"Yeah, yeah. So how's work going?"

"By the way, I saw you on the news and forgot to call you. I never knew you were that deep into airplane shit."

"Yeah, I guess you could say I'm pretty deep."

"You're a god damn government agent. No wonder you live in a palace."

"Wanna trade? You go sift through the ashes and wreckage of a burned up plane full of dead bodies and I'll be the musician."

"Aww come on, Logan that's gross."

"That's what I do."

"Ew."

"Haha."

"Anyway, I didn't just call to see if JT was any good, I wanted to know if you get any kind of vacation."

"No. Not really. Why?"

"I'm going to Key West this coming weekend for Women's Fest. We're playing Friday and Saturday night. You should come down and party with us."

"Hmm, that does sound like a good idea. I don't exactly get a vacation but I can work my schedule so that I can take Friday and Monday out of the office. I'm on call twenty four hours a day, seven days a week."

"That blows."

"I'm use to it."

"So are you in?"

"Sure."

"Should I expect you to be alone?" Lynnie questioned.

"Of course, I'm sure she'll be there, but I doubt we will actually ride together and stay in a hotel together the whole weekend. It's not like that."

"Right, I forgot you're just fucking."

"My god Lynnie, do you have to be so vulgar?"

"Well it's true. Don't be such a grouch Logan."

"Yes, but we *have* actually dated a little bit and I'm not a grouch!"

"Okay okay."

***

Logan rushed her week along, sitting through conference call after conference call. Then she flew to Washington for two days of meetings at NTSB Headquarters, desperately trying to avoid the one person that turned her world upside down. She ended her week early and drove the seven and a half hour trip to Key West, Florida. She met up with Lynnie and her band at the hotel and went straight to the bar to help them set up.

The band started up around eight o'clock, not long after, Logan noticed Jensen walk into the bar. They immediately made eye contact and Jensen worked her way over to Logan.

"Hey, stranger." Jensen leaned in for short seductive kiss.

"Did you just get here?"

"Yeah, I had to work and then I hit traffic coming down."

"That sucks."

"Yeah, my friends are coming down tomorrow. They didn't want to drive down after work today."

They drank a few beers together, listened to Lynnie jam on her slide guitar with her blues band, and partied with her between sets. Before they knew it, it was four a.m. Jensen went back to her hotel and Logan promised to meet her for brunch.

Logan woke up before the alarm went off, surprised that she wasn't hung over. She took a quick shower and headed down to the café on Duval Street to meet Jensen. She walked into the small establishment and noticed Jensen had company, another blond that could pass as Logan's twin sister.

"Good Morning." Logan bent and kissed Jensen's cheek before she sat down.

"Hey. Logan this is Megan."

"Hi, it's nice to meet you." Logan reached across the table to shake the girl's hand.

They all ordered food and coffee. Logan wondered who this mysterious friend was since she wasn't with Jensen last night and she'd never seen her before.

"So what's your plan for the day?" Logan asked between sips of coffee.

"I think we're going to do a little shopping and then hit the pool before we do the 'Duval crawl'."

"That sounds like a plan."

"I'm going up to Islamorada with Lynnie to look at some property that she wants to buy and then we're hitting the bars."

"It's nice up there. I'd love to live down here in the keys."

"Yeah me too, but my job would never allow it."

"I doubt mine would either."

"Call me later, maybe we can meet up for dinner or something."

"I'm not sure where I'll be, but I'll call you if I'm around for dinner. I'm sure I'll see you in the bar tonight. Isn't Lynnie playing?"

"Yeah, she's on from eight until two. I believe

126

she's playing two sets tonight."

"Sounds good."

***

Logan spent the rest of the afternoon hanging out with Lynnie. She wasted a good hour talking Lynnie out of buying a shit piece of property. Then she showed her a much nicer piece of actual real estate that was worth the asking amount, but much pricier than Lynnie wanted to pay. They decided to call it a day and hit the bar before the band started. Jensen never called Logan about dinner, so Logan called her from the bar and got her voicemail. The band started up at eight and Logan noticed Jensen walk in with the same girl that she was with that morning, except this time they were all over each other. Logan turned towards the bartender.

"Double shot of Patron please ma'am." She downed the shot to help calm her nerves before she made her way through the crowd towards Jensen. Logan stopped directly in front of her.

"What's going on here?"

"Hey, what's up?"

"Jensen, what the hell?" Logan ran her eyes to the other woman and back to Jensen.

"What's your problem?"

"Well I'd like to know if you wanted to fuck other people."

"Whoa calm down, it's not like I'm your girlfriend. So we had a few good times, I'm not exclusive with anyone."

"Oh is that a fact, what an asshole! I never wanted to be exclusive either, but you could at least give me a fucking heads up if you plan on fucking other people."

"Hey, don't talk to her like that." The mini-me chimed in.

"Miss Thing, I suggest you butt right the fuck back out of this conversation." She turned back towards the woman who acted as if nothing was wrong. "Fuck you Jensen. I wasn't looking to get played."

"Hey, you should've heard about me in the bar. I'm sorry if you didn't know how I was."

Logan walked back towards the bar and ordered another double shot of Patron'. Lynnie had finished her first set and went straight over to Logan.

"What the hell was that all about? Who's that girl?"

"I got played. That's her new bitch!" Logan downed the glass.

"Oh man, Logan, honey I'm sorry. I thought you knew how she was."

"Nope apparently I missed the fucking memo!"

"She's fucked up Logan, I mean she's still married and shit. All she does is fuck different girls."

"She's married?"

"Opps."

"Lynnie!"

"Sorry, I thought you knew. She's married to some guy. She left him and moved to Florida a while ago. She's finally getting a divorce or so I heard. She says she's a lesbian but she won't get serious with any girl. All she does is fuck them and move on."

"Damn it, why the hell do I always get mixed up with the fucking loony tunes! I swear I'm going to be celibate for the rest of my life. I'm through with women. Bartender, another double, baby keep 'em coming."

Fate Vs. Destiny

"What are you drinking?"

"Patron."

"Holy shit, this will be a long night. Better make that two!"

***

By the time Lynnie went back on stage to start her second set, her and Logan had put away three double shots each. Lynnie was beginning to feel a buzz and Logan was past drunk, but handling it rather well considering she didn't care anymore.

"I need to ask a good friend of mine to come up here and help me with a few cover songs in this set. Logan, get your sexy ass up here."

Logan's eyes turned dark blue and grew large as she shook her head no.

"Aw come on, we both know you can sing."

"No Lynnie!" Logan tried not to make a scene.

The crowd starting chanting for her to go sing and Logan gave in. She stopped to whisper in Lynnie's ear as she got up on stage. "I'm gonna beat your ass for this!"

"I might like it!" Lynnie countered with a smile.

***

The band started soft, as Lynnie chimed in with her slide guitar Logan began pouring out the words to one of her favorite songs and ironically, the song that her and Jensen danced to the night they met.

The crowd started cheering for Logan and Lynnie's deep blues rendition of Ottis Reddings' *Sittin' on the Doc of the Bay*. By the time the song was over the

129

whole bar was watching Logan's every move and singing along with her and Lynnie.

"Looks like you have an audience." Lynnie whispered in Logan's ear. The crowd was cheering for her to continue singing.

Too drunk to realize what she was doing, Logan fired back with "What's next?"

Lynnie winked, smiled, and started playing her slide guitar in a slow tune. Then the band answered back with an upbeat tune. Logan immediately knew what they were playing. She smiled seductively as she boldly started the lyrics to *I Touch Myself* by The Vinyls.

At the end of that song Logan went back to the bar for another round while Lynnie sang a few of her own songs. Later on when she was ready to end the night, she called Logan back to the stage to sing again. The band's deep melody and Lynnie's strong-willed slide guitar, were the background to a perfect blues harmony as Logan and Lynnie began their absolute favorite song together, *Get it While You Can* by Howard Tate.

Most of the women in the bar had partnered up and began dancing halfway through the song. Lynnie and Logan sang the soul-searching blues song with profound emotion. No one noticed that it was actually to each other, one trying to help out a sad friend with some advice and the other telling her friend what she was going through.

***

Lynnie was packing up her equipment when she saw Jensen walk by with her new flame.

"I hope she's worth it." She snarled.

Fate Vs. Destiny

Jensen tucked her chin and ignored the slur. Lynnie finished and headed back to the hotel. She found Logan lying in a lawn chair on the pool deck, starring up at the stars. The tears had already dried on her cheeks.

"What's up?" Lynnie lay in the chair next to her.

"Not much, my head hurts like hell."

"I'd say so, you pretty much finished off more than a pint of Patron' straight up. I don't think I've ever seen you drink like that."

"Damn, no wonder I feel like shit." Logan rubbed her tired eyes.

"Uh huh."

"What a fucked up night."

"You can say that again. I still can't believe that tramp did that to you."

"C'est la vie! Lynnie, C'est la vie!"

"What the hell does that mean?"

"That's life."

***

They woke up a few hours later when the sun came up, still in the deck chairs. Logan looked great but felt like death twice over. Lynnie wasn't in as bad a shape, but not up for a marathon either. She looked over at her friend and started laughing.

"What the fuck are you laughing at?" Logan spat out.

"A government agent with a broken heart that spent the night drunk in a pool chair."

"Thanks Lynnie, I love you too! By the way, you look like hell."

"Have you seen yourself?"

131

"I bet you'll look better wet!" Lynnie said as she jumped up and dumped Logan into the pool with her chair. Logan grabbed her before she could catch her balance and Lynnie fell in on top of the chair. Both women swam to the surface splashing and cursing each other, meanwhile laughing hysterically. "I was right. You're sexy when you're wet!"

"Lynnie I look like a drowned rat!" Her tee shirt and jeans were stuck to her.

"I know!"

Logan slapped her arm. "Shut up."

Both women climbed out of the pool, thankful that it was too early in the morning for any of the other hotel guests to be out around the pool area. Logan was relieved to see her cell phone sitting on the table where the chairs use to be.

"Come on. I need some coffee."

"Like this? Hell no!"

"Logan, who gives a flying fuck what you look like. Do you really care if you see any of these people again?"

"For once Lynnie…you're right." Both women headed down the street to the café, neither giving a care in the world to the oddball stares and comments coming from passers by.

***

"What time are you leaving?"

"Probably as soon as I get back and shower. What about you?"

"Yeah, I'm right behind you. I need to make sure the guys made it back last night then I'm out of here."

"Are you stopping in Islamorada?"

"Nah, I'll come back in a few months and look again. I'm not in any big hurry, plus I have to sell my house too."

***

Logan arrived back home, stripped out of her clothes, went straight to her king-size bed, and passed out. She bypassed unpacking her suitcase, checking her email, and eating dinner.

The hibernating woman flew out of the bed at five a.m. when her alarm went off.

"Ah...damn job!" She screeched as she stepped into the steaming hot shower.

She checked her email before she left for the office. In three short days she had acquired over fifty emails.

***

Logan spent most of her day in her office on conference calls. She was well aware that she had to be in Washington, D.C. for a meeting at the end of the week. She was desperately searching for a reason to fail to attend. She worked until nine o'clock and finally decided to give up on the pile of paperwork on her desk and go home. Ricky, the security guard walked her to the airport exit. He always made it a point to converse with her. It always made her day to talk to him since he always seemed positive.

***

133

Logan spent the rest of her week sitting through meeting after meeting and phone call after phone call, until Friday morning. Her flight arrived at Washington's Dulles Airport at eight a.m., just in time for her to make her nine o'clock meeting at the NTSB Headquarters building. *If these flights get any tighter I swear I'll miss one of these meetings one day, then what?* The fair headed bombshell, dressed in a black pants suit and a baby blue blouse, turned heads as usual when she walked into the conference room on the fifth floor. She stopped to speak to a few people, quick to ignore the beautiful agent sitting on the corner representing the FAA and staring a hole through her.

The meeting lasted five and half hours with a short lunch break in the middle. As soon as it was over, Logan was on her way out the door to hail a taxi instead of waiting for a ride with the rest of the group in the corporate limo. Brooke was quick on her heels.

"Are you even going to say hi to me?"

"Nope." Logan never looked at her as she got into the yellow car and rode off.

***

Two agonizing weeks later Logan was laying on her couch on a Friday night watching TV and drinking a smooth chilled glass of Navan, when her house phone rang. Considering she only has it so that the front desk can call her to let a visitor come up, she jumped up and answered it.

"Hi Miss Greer, this is Juan at the front desk. I'm sorry to bother you this late, I have a guest named Brooke

McCabe here to see you."

"What? Uh…tell her I'm busy." *Why the hell is she here?*

"Yes Ma'am."

Five minutes later the phone rang again.

"Hi Miss Greer, I'm sorry to bother you again, but Miss McCabe says that it is very urgent that you see her."

"Tell her I'm asleep, Juan, think of something. Don't call me again." *Goddamn her.*

Five more minutes went by and her cell phone rang. It was a Washington number so she had to answer it since she had Brooke in her caller ID and her name didn't show up.

"Agent Greer."

"Don't hang up Logan."

"Brooke damn it I don't want to talk to you or see you or whatever else you have in mind so you might as well go back home."

"Please let me come up. I need to talk to you."

"I have nothing to say to you."

"I don't want to do this on the phone in the lobby."

"Good me either. Good bye." Logan slammed the phone shut, downed the glass of cognac, and walked out onto the balcony. *The nerve of that woman coming to my house! Damn you, Brooke, I'll never get over you unless you leave me alone!* Seconds went by before she was back inside pouring herself another glass, she walked back out on the balcony after she downed the vanilla flavored liquid. The night was clear and breezy. The sky was lit up by a full moon surrounded by millions of brightly shinning stars. "Nothing like a broken heart on a beautiful night, huh Greer."

Nine

Left...right...left,...right...right,...right,...right, left...right,...left. The sweat rolled from her blond brow, down her face, dripping from her chin to the smooth muscles contracting in her stomach as she pounded the heavy bag. She spent the past three weeks working out every free second she found, desperately trying to remove every emotional memory of the woman that had shattered her heart. Just before her vigorous workout routine ended her cell phone rang loudly. She struggled to shed the boxing gloves before answering.

"Greer."

"Agent Greer, this is Walter Hudson with the NTSB Aviation Department in D.C."

"Yes Sir."

"A 747 went down off the coast of California just after takeoff from LAX."

"How long ago?"

"It was reported to us ten minutes ago, but it disappeared from radar approximately one hour ago. I've booked you on a private jet leaving from JIA in an hour. You should arrive at LAX by nine a.m. There will be a rental car there for you to drive down to the Seal Beach Naval Weapons Station in Seal Beach. There's a Coast Guard Cutter stationed there that's working the recovery. Your team should meet you at the dock."

Fate Vs. Destiny

"I'm on my way to the airport now, Sir. I'll let you know when I land." *Shit, not a UW. Underwater investigation is so time-consuming and rigorous. There goes my schedule for the next few months.* She thought to herself as she quickly showered and headed for the door. *Here we go again.*

***

Logan dressed in jeans and a dark blue sweatshirt with NTSB in large yellow letters on the back, a white tee shirt underneath, and black doc martens. She rounded up her team on the dock while they waited for the ship to return for them. She recognized most of the members from other accidents that she had worked. Brooke was also on scene, standing in the back with the rest of her group, just close enough to hear her ex-lover speak.

"Listen up ladies and gentlemen. We have a tremendously extreme situation here. This plane is sitting on the bottom of the ocean floor and has been for the past four hours. The only information that we have at this time is there are no survivors and the wreckage is sitting twenty miles off the coast of Long Beach, 250 meters down, in forty-five degree water. There are very few clues as to why this plane may have gone down. It is my job along with the help of all of you to determine the cause of this fatal catastrophe. The Coast Guard Cutter Ship that we will be on is small compared to the amount of people that we will have working together. I'm going to need part of the FAA and NTSB teams to set up an operations area in one of the hangars here on base along with the Coast Guard and NOAA to send and receive information to and from the ship.

"We will work around the clock with the Navy Divers until ninety-five percent of the wreckage has been recovered. Myself, as well as, five others will be on the boat at all times for the first few days or so. The rest of you will come out with us in shifts of five at a time on a small utility boat every couple of hours. Let me warn you now, it will be cold, wet, and miserable out there. If you get sea sick at all please tell me now so I can make sure you have a position on dry land. The rest of you need to put the sea sick patch behind your right ear so that you have no problems out on the water. The last time I worked on a UW we went from calm to five foot seas within a half hour and trust me the boat stays out there, so you better be able to handle it."

***

The small Utility boat pulled up along the dock. Two Coast Guard Petty Officer's stepped off to help Logan's team board with their equipment and to brief Logan before she made it on scene.

Once on board the Cutter Ship, Logan pulled Brooke aside while they were still below deck. Both women spoke professionally.

"We need to work together on this. The first three days are the most critical."

"I know that, I don't want to be out here any longer than you do. Trust me."

Logan felt a throbbing pain in the pit of her stomach as she followed Brooke into the navigation room next to the wheelhouse. They needed to speak to the Captain and go over the topography scans from the Side Scanning Radar that was taking pictures of the debris field on the ocean floor. *Working next to you like this is the hardest thing I have ever had to do.*

***

The pictures showed the plane broken up into three large blobs. Smaller pieces were scattered as far as the sonar could scan. Logan knew she had a hell of a long investigation ahead of her.

"Captain Warner, we need to recover this entire plane as quickly as possible. Every hour of time we waste in recovery causes multiple delayed hours in our investigation. It's critical that each and every piece be handled with extreme caution. These broken water logged fragments are all we have to solve this case with."

"Yes Ma'am." The tall, brown haired man spoke with a deep voice.

***

For the first week Logan and Brooke supervised and labored around the clock, watching, recovering, and logging every item that the divers brought to the surface, from pieces of plane, to items of clothing and luggage, even human remains. She worked next to the woman she hated because she had to. Nothing ever stood in the way of her job, not even Brooke.

By the end of the first week all of the bodies had been retrieved. The debris was put onto a barge that was towed back to the Navy base twice daily. Back on the base, part of the FAA and NTSB crews worked continuously, soaking every piece in fresh water, and then drying it as part of their job rebuilding the plane in the hangar and analyzing every piece of wreckage. The other half of the group interviewed witnesses and airport employees that handled the planes maintenance before it departed. Neither woman spoke of their involvement, instead they remained on a highly professional level.

The second week had gone by out on the ship. The complete fuselage, both wings, all four engines, and the tail were recovered and sitting in the hangar at Seal Beach Naval Weapons Station. The divers were still bringing hundreds of smaller sections of the aircraft to the surface one piece at a time. The FAA and NTSB crews moved off of the ship and began working in the hangar. Logan was standing outside talking to one of her assistants when her cell phone vibrated in her pocket. Brooke was standing close by nonchalantly watching her while they worked.

"Agent Greer." Logan answered in a grouchy hoarse voice.

"Is this the good-looking Agent that's cranky because she's been out on a ship in the cold water all week?"

Logan smiled and her voice calmed to a much friendlier tone. She immediately recognized the voice of her ex-wife and best friend.

"Hey. I haven't talked to you in a while. You must have ESP."

"I saw the news and figured I had a hundred percent chance that you'd be here for that plane crash."

"Yeah, how can I resist?"

Brooke watched the interaction as Logan continued talking, smiling, and laughing with whoever was on the other end. She hid the burning jealousy in her chest and the pit of her stomach.

140

"So how busy are you? Will you have time to see me before you take off?"

"I'm up to my asshole in soaking wet airplane fragments, but I can always make time to see you."

"Good, I'm making my Mom's Teriyaki Shrimp and Chicken with Scalloped Potatoes. You have to come by for dinner."

"Mm, that sounds great! You always did know the way to my stomach! I'll see you around eight." Logan closed her phone and went around the corner to go back into the hangar. She noticed Brooke off to the side, part of her wanted to go talk to her, but none of her knew where to begin. Every time Brooke spoke a word, the painful heartache came rushing back to her. *Why can't I let you go?*

***

Logan stepped into the elevator on her way out of the hotel. Brooke was already in there. She looked up and down at the woman in front of her curiously.

"Hey."

Logan nodded back.

"Hot date?"

Logan didn't acknowledge the comment.

"Logan you could at least speak to me. Do you hate me that much?" Brooke's heart ached as she spoke.

"I'm going to see Chaney. She lives in L.A."

"Isn't that your ex-wife?"

"Yeah."

"Oh."

The doors opened and Logan was the first one out. She never looked back as she left the building.

***

Forty-five minutes later, Logan pulled up at large Condo tower. She went inside and took the elevator up to the third floor. Chaney opened when she knocked on the door.

"Hey there."

"Right back at ya!" They hugged for a long second.

"How've you been?" Chaney brought Logan inside and showed her around her three bedroom, two bath condo.

"Great, my show's taking off faster than I can keep up. I haven't had any time to do stand up at night. The clubs keep calling, but by the time I get home I need to work on my lines for the next morning."

"That's awesome; you look like you're really happy. I know how it is working your ass off. Sometimes I get home when the sun's coming up, I have enough time to shower and change before I have to go back. But, I love what I do."

"Hey speaking of happy, what's up? You look as exhausted as I feel."

"I've been working around the clock for two weeks on this investigation. You know how I get."

"Yeah, I know how you are and I've seen you when you're buried in your work, but you just don't look like yourself."

"I'm fine Chaney."

"Okay. Want a beer?"

"Do you have anything stronger?"

"Um…Captain Morgan, Crown, Patron'..."

"Patron on the rocks."

Chaney took a second and looked at the person that knew her inside and out. She knew Logan was lying to her, she could see right through the façade. If the sadness in her eyes didn't give it away, the stiff drink order definitely did.

After dinner they sat on the couch. Logan never talked about work. She didn't think anyone should hear about the things she sees. Chaney was bored discussing her own job so they talked about old times.

"So what's new with your life these days, are you dating?"

"No. Just working."

"Do you still see Lynnie?"

"Of course, I see her every couple of weeks we usually go to the bar or dinner."

"I always thought you guys would get together."

"Lynnie, and me? No way. She's a good friend and we all know she'd hook up with me if I blinked twice, but I don't get with my friends and she's not what I'm looking for."

"Uh huh and what is it that you are looking for?"

"Hell I don't even know. I'm not even looking."

"Aw, poor baby, I should introduce you to some friends."

"Gross, Chaney, I'm your ex-wife. You really wanna hook me up with one of your friends?"

"True, bad idea."

"Besides, I'm not looking. I don't have time for women."

"You're not messing with men are you?"

Logan smacked her arm.

"Hell no!"

143

"Come on Logan, I've known you for a long time. I probably know you better than anyone. What's going on with you?"

"I …well…over a year ago I met someone and it was basically a fling here or there. I haven't bothered with anyone since."

"What happened? Who is she?"

"She's an investigator for the FAA. We basically had a hot office affair and hooked up when we saw each other for meetings or investigations."

"Okay…"

"For a while there were no strings attached, a lot like friends with benefits. You know hot sex and nothing else. Then one night she was in Jacksonville working and asked me to show her my home. After that night we went from hot steamy sex to making love to each other. Everything changed between us when I let her into my life."

"I'm happy for you."

"Don't be, a few months ago I found out that she's engaged to one of the leads for TSA Homeland Security. A good looking Italian… MAN!" Her voice was thick with animosity.

"Oh my god, Logan!" Chaney was shocked.

"Yeah you're telling me. Anyway, I've been a mess since I found out. She even came to my house to talk to me and I wouldn't let her in. Now she's here with me working and it's driving me crazy."

"I'm so sorry. That's terrible."

"Leave it to me to get involved with a straight woman," Logan sighed.

"You love her don't you?"

"What…I …" She took a long pause, trying not to

admit it. "I love her and I hate her so god damn much."

Chaney leaned over and held Logan.

"I know how hard it is. When we split up I hated you for choosing your career and pushing me away, but I loved you with all of my heart for making me follow my own career, so I let you go. Everything happens for a reason. I was never able to do anything with my comedy until I was all alone, now look at me."

"Yeah, I'm so proud of you. I miss you a lot. It sucks not being close to you anymore. I hate having my best friend across the country."

"Me too!"

Chaney took a chance. She always knew what to say whether or not Logan wanted to hear it was a different story. "Go after her Logan, follow your heart. I'm sure she loves you too, especially if she's trying to explain herself to you. Who knows what she has to say."

"She's still with him. They're getting married."

"There has to be a reason why she's trying to talk to you, I'm sure she's having a hard time too."

"Every time I hear her voice I want to hold her in my arms and beat the hell out of something at the same time."

"You're hurting. Honey, you need to get past it somehow."

"I know. I've never been torn up like this over anything Chaney. I can't eat, can't sleep. Being out on that boat with her is driving me nuts. Her god damn scent sticks to everything, I smell her everywhere. It's like the plague!"

"Aw…Go to her Logan. Listen to what she has to say. Do it because you love her and you deserve to know the truth."

"How did you get so good at advice? You use to hide behind your feelings. What the hell happened to you?"

"The opposite of you, I guess." They both laughed and sat back against the couch."

"I think my drink needs a refill"

"Hey mine too while you're at it!"

They continued to drink and talk for a few more hours. Logan passed out in the spare room.

***

Another week started in the investigation. Logan continued to ignore Brooke, unless it pertained to the case. Together they sifted through every piece of water-logged wreckage. Separately they worked on their own conclusions. Both women were still unable to rule out a terrorist attack and this caused chaos in the news day in and day out. Towards the end of the week Logan walked into the hanger, slash investigation headquarters as usual. The tiny blonde hairs on the back of her neck stood on end when she heard a familiar voice close by, as she turned the corner she ran slap into Mathew Taglia. Brooke appeared behind him less than a second later.

"Good afternoon."

Logan remained professional. Part of her wanted to kill him, but the other part of her realized he was just as clueless as she had been.

"Mr. Taglia." *Well if it isn't the happy fucking couple.*

"Agent Greer." He smiled at Logan as he spoke. *Oh my god, she never told him. What a bitch!*

"Brooke, uh...I have a conference call in an hour

with Boeing, you should probably sit in on the call with me. We need to try to get some kind of lead way with this."

Ten

After the meeting ended with the Boeing Safety Committee, Logan jumped into her SUV and headed towards the other side of the military base to meet the ocean. She was completely unaware that Brooke was following closely on her heels. When the vehicle came to rest Logan stepped out into the sand and began walking. Not knowing how long or how far she'd walked, she turned around to hit the automatic lock on her key chain. That's when she noticed the similar looking black SUV pull up next to hers. Brooke looked like an angel bathed in sunlight as she got out and walked towards the sand. *Damn you Brooke, why can't you just leave me alone?*

"I need to talk to you, Logan."

"This is not the time nor the place." Logan kept walking.

"Damn it listen to me, there will never be a right time or place. I'm so sorry I hurt you." Brooke was hot on her heels, practically running to keep up with her.

"Give me a fucking break! You never even told him!" Logan stopped and turned to face the tiny figure behind her.

"Don't talk to me like that…I can't tell him."

"Why not, he deserves to know. Or, was I not suppose to find out either?"

Brooke's eyes swelled as the tears began falling. Her voice cracked softly.

"I never meant to hurt you, Logan."

"Yeah, well you should have thought of that."

"That's just it. I wasn't thinking at all with you." She tried to choke back the tears but they fell anyway.

"What made you do it Brooke? Why did you come after me when you were already with him?"

"I don't know. I guess something is always missing in my life. I met you and you couldn't stand me, but I was intrigued by you."

"So you led me on because you were intrigued? What was missing in your relationship? What made you look to a woman?" Logan was pissed and upset at the same time.

"Nothing and everything all at the same time. I don't know, Logan. I…we…you are an amazing person. Once I started I couldn't stop. I fell in love with you."

"So what's missing when you're with me then, if something is always missing in your life?" Logan ignored the words the tore at her heart.

"Nothing…and it scares the hell out of me."

"Why does it scare you Brooke? I don't understand."

"Because it's so different, you're so different, we're so different. I think about you a thousand times a day. I miss you so much."

"Then why are you with him?"

"Because a part of me loves him too and wants to get married and have a normal life."

Logan turned her head to hide the tears in her eyes. She stared at the sun connecting with the ocean. Slowly she started walking down the beach again. Brooke walked along just behind her.

"Did you ever picture your life with me instead?" Logan's anger turned to sadness.

"I think about it all the time. I see us happy, until the holidays come around or it comes time to have children."

"So you stay with him because of society, your family, and the fact that you want kids? That is seriously fucked up Brooke. You're thirty two years old, grow up!" Sadness now turned back to anger.

"This is where I belong."

"You have no idea. You say you love me and a part of you is missing when you're with him and you've found that part along with everything else when you're with me. Yet you chose to be unhappy. I don't understand it."

"I am happy with him."

"Oh really, well something sent you to me and it wasn't just sex. You're in love with me Brooke. Can't you see how much I love you too?" Logan couldn't believe what she just said. It was true, she was in love with her, but it hurt her to say it.

"I know. This is a choice that I will question and I will wonder about you and miss you for the rest of my life."

"So that's it?"

"You said you never want to see me again. Except for work I guess."

"I need to forget about you and move on with my life. You turned my world upside down."

The tears were streaming down Brooke's face. Logan clinched her fists until she could swear they were bleeding, but she held her composure, refusing to break down in front of this woman.

"I'm so sorry, Logan, I never meant to hurt you. I'll let you go so you can forget about me and everything we had."

"Goodbye." Logan turned away as Brooke walked back up the beach towards their cars. She waited a few minutes, then plopped down in the sand to let the tears roll from her eyes. She sat on that beach crying like a baby into the arms of the sunset.

***

A few short hours later Logan found herself still in her business suit sitting on a stool in 'Main St. Blues', a semi-familiar bar that she passed through a year ago. The same older looking female bartender stopped in front of her.

"I never thought I'd see you in here again. You still look like you're lost. What'll it be?"

Lady you have no idea. How about Brooke's head on a platter? Do you think you can do that? Wait, what about holding my gun to my head for me so I can pull the trigger? I can't seem to hold it there myself. How about something to end this god damn misery that I'm stuck in? Can you serve me something that will make it all disappear? Here's a better idea, make her disappear...no wait...me...make me disappear. "Glass of Navan on the rocks. Please."

"That's a pretty strong order. Good stuff though. Wish I could handle it myself."

The woman returned seconds later with the vanilla flavored, transparent gold colored liquid. Logan downed half of the glass before the woman could step away.

"Who are you trying to forget, honey?"

Logan didn't speak. Her ears were tuned to the blues band on the stage playing old Otis Redding songs.

"He must be one asshole of a man to break your heart...twice."

Just as the woman finished her sentence the TV in the corner was displaying the nightly news. They happened to be discussing terrorism and showing images of the plane crash and the latest press conference. Logan's face was plastered all over the TV along with Brooke, the California Mayor, and a few military officials. The older woman turned back towards the blonde at the end of the bar. Logan had turned her head away from the screen.

God damn stupid ass news people have no fucking clue...

"It's on the house tonight, honey." Logan hadn't noticed the bartender come back over to her with another round after she changed the channel. She merely nodded her head in appreciation as she grabbed the glass.

A very attractive brunette in a black skirt suit moved down to Logan's end of the bar.

"Mind if I join you?"

Logan shrugged her shoulders and went back drinking the ice cold Cognac as the woman sat on the stool.

"I saw you on the TV, no wonder you're drinking toilet water."

Logan turned towards the woman. "Excuse me?"

She laughed softly. "When I was young my mother used to call straight hard liquor, toilet water and said it would kill me so I shouldn't drink it when I grew up."

Logan nodded and continued to swallow the 'toilet water'.

"I know you're not a mute, I saw you talking on the TV."

"And?"

"What's your name? Hi, how are you? Blah, blah, blah."

"I'm really not in the mood for conversation tonight." *Ugh...put a fucking sock in it go-go gadget mouth! Get the hint and leave me the hell alone!*

The seductive brunette leaned over to Logan's ear. "I don't usually do this but, I think you're unbelievably hot."

"That's nice."

"I've never been with a woman. I have no idea why I'm doing this."

Logan finished her glass and nodded down to the bartender for another. "Look, I'm flattered...really. But, I'm not here to pick anyone up and I'd really prefer to be alone right now."

The seductive woman slid a business card over to Logan as she stood up and walked away.

My god, what the hell is wrong with straight woman? Do I have a sign on my forehead that says 'I fuck straight women...only'?

Two more glasses later, Logan grabbed her cell phone and hit speed dial number one.

"Hello?"

"Hey, Chaney."

"Logan, what's up?"

"Uh...do you know where 'Main St. Blues' is?"

"Yeah?"

153

"Would you mind coming to get me? I probably shouldn't drive."

"I'm on the way."

Chaney saw Logan immediately when she entered the tiny local bar.

"Hey stranger."

"Hi."

"Uh oh, Logan you look like shit. What happened?"

"I'll tell you in the car." Logan tossed a fifty on the bar and nodded at the bartender as she exited with Chaney.

***

Logan told Chaney about her conversation with Brooke in the car. They both decided she should spend the night in Chaney's spare room and go back for her SUV in the morning. Logan met her beautiful ex-wife on the couch waiting for her with a hot cup of coffee.

"I can't believe she said that shit to you. What an asshole. No wonder you're drunk!"

"Yeah, you're telling me. I'm getting to the point where I can see through the alcohol."

"Honey I'm sorry I told you to talk to her. You deserve so much better than that bitch."

"It's not your fault. Its karma…she bites my ass every fucking chance she gets."

"It has to be hard for you to work with her."

"Oh you have no idea…Everything reminds me of her. Everything smells like her. It's driving me crazy! I'm in love with her and I hate her…god I hate her so much."

"I know you do."

"I'll be glad when this investigation's over...I won't have to see her everyday. I want to knock her head off, I swear."

"I can't believe she didn't tell him. That's really fucked up."

"I know. What a fucking chicken! She kept telling me she was scared. Scared to start over, scared of what her family would think, scared of things not working out between us."

"She's going to live the rest of her life scared, Logan. Unfortunately there's nothing you can do about it. She has to get over society and her family before she can be strong enough to let herself love you."

"Yeah well that'll never happen."

"True, I wouldn't hold my breath. Hey, you want some more coffee?"

"Sure, I'm going to have one hell of a hang over in the morning."

"Yup."

***

Chaney came back to the couch with two more cups of coffee.

"I still don't understand how she could play with your emotions like that and then act like its all okay."

Logan chuckled.

"It's actually happened twice."

"Huh, what do you mean?"

"Right before I met Brooke, I met another girl one night at the bar close to my house. We didn't sleep together but she came close to taking me home. Not long after that I met Brooke and things happened with us. I

155

still saw the other girl once in a while, but nothing happened."

"Okay…"

"After things went sour with me and Brooke I ran into the girl again and I finally went home with her. We sort of dated for a few weeks. My heart wasn't in it, but the sex was fairly good."

Chaney laughed. "Okay."

"I went to the Keys with Lynnie and she was supposed to meet me down there since she was also going with friends. Long story short, the bitch showed up with another girl, and basically told me to my face that she's a player, and too bad."

"What the hell?"

"Yeah go figure."

"Logan, where do you find these girls?!"

"At work and in a bar."

"You have really pissed Karma off; she is after your ass."

"No shit! I'm just not going to have sex anymore. I'm damn sure never falling in love again. My heart is in a million tiny pieces and every time I see Brooke she stomps all over them."

"Aw I really am sorry, Logan. You deserve so much better."

"Coming from you Chaney, that means a lot to me."

Chaney leaned over and hugged Logan.

***

Chaney woke Logan right after the sun came up so that she could go get her vehicle. Logan went straight to her hotel to shower and change before going to the hangar. When she arrived she noticed that Brooke was already there knee deep in paperwork. Logan's head was pounding and she swore she could smell alcohol on herself.

Logan you really need to get the ball rolling so you can wrap up this investigation...God, I'm so sick of seeing her everyday I don't know how much more of it I can take, especially seeing her with him. I'm liable to puke on them both. I bet he's never touched you like I did...Damn it Logan don't even think about it. All you're doing is hurting yourself. Two months of this and I'm going crazy! The inner-self conversation continued as Logan passed Brooke's desk on the way to her own.

Bitch...Don't even look at me. I might slap you. Oh and you can stop wearing the short skirts, they will get you nowhere with me!

As soon as she sat in her chair her Systems Recovery Analyst came around the corner.

"Agent Greer, we found the black box. The CVR and the FDR are both soaking in fresh water. We should be able to analyze them within the hour."

"Good, let me know as soon as we're ready."

"Yes, ma'am."

***

Logan made a few calls to Washington and completed some paperwork before she listened to the CVR and then read the computer analysis of the FDR. Brooke was standing right next to her doing the same thing as part of her job. Logan met with her team and Brooke met with hers to discuss their findings. A few

157

hours later Logan called Brooke into her office.

"We've recovered ninety-two percent of this plane, including, the most crucial parts. It's quite obvious there was a mechanical failure. We heard the pilot and co-pilot when the engines stalled. The FDR shows that just after take off they lost oil pressure in the left engine. As soon as they cut the engine and decided to turn back towards the airport the right engine went out. The plane immediately went into a nose dive and struck the water within seconds. Is this the same conclusion that you've come to? Or do you have anything to add?"

Brooke went through her notes. "No, my report is almost verbatim."

"Good, I'm calling a conference in an hour with Washington to submit my on-scene conclusion. I'm sure we will have another go around with the press before we wrap up here."

"Yeah."

"I'll expect you to be on the podium with me and the Mayor again. I'll call your cell when I have a time scheduled."

"Okay."

***

Logan spent three hours talking to her boss, his boss, and so on up the ladder. She went through every major piece of evidence that led her to her conclusion. She received the go ahead to end the on-site investigation and release her findings to the press, mostly to stop the terrorism hype that the media started.

Four hours later she had appeared on the news, held two meetings, said good-bye to Chaney once again, and was now boarding a plane headed home.

"Good afternoon, Agent. May I get you anything?" The young-looking flight attendant grinned as she spoke the words.

One corner of Logan's mouth curled slightly in a half-assed smile.

"No thank you, I'm fine."

"Yes you are." The young woman mumbled under her breath but loud enough for Logan to hear.

Wow why don't you just invite me to the lavatory in fifteen minutes? I could use some more 'Mile High Club' miles. God just let me get home to my time zone, climb into my bed, and move on with my life.

***

The plane landed on time. Logan stopped in her office to check her messages with her secretary and arrange some kind of order for the following week. She was in her truck and heading towards her Condo in Jacksonville Beach before she knew it. Just as she pulled through the gates her cell phone rattled against her belt as it rang loudly. *Goddamn it.*

"Greer."

"Hey, how're they hanging?" The scratchy voice laughed.

"Hey Lynnie, what's up?"

"Are you back in town yet?"

"As a matter of fact I just pulled up at home."

"Great! I'm headed your way. I should be there within thirty minutes."

"What…wait Lynnie you're headed here? Why?"

"We're going out."

"We are?"

"Hell yeah, you've been gone for like two months and my band is home from the tour this weekend so me and you are painting the beach, baby."

"I see."

"Get dressed. I'll call you when I get there."

"Uh…okay…"

Lynnie hung up the phone before Logan could turn her down or come up with some sort of excuse for why she didn't want to go out or do anything for that matter, except beat the hell out of the punching bag and run on the beach under the stars. *Damnit Lynnie! There's noway I can begin to tell you about Brooke. You'll never understand. Cheer up Logan you old bloat!*

***

They walked into the local Irish Pub, both wearing jeans, and flip flops. Logan was in a canary yellow polo with baby blue stripes that accented her light colored hair and Lynnie was in a white tee shirt. It was still early on Friday night so they were able to get a free space at the bar. Hoping for the cute female bartender with the skin tight tee shirt on, they were saddened to see the tall broad male with spiky hair coming their way.

"Evening ladies. What'll it be?"

Logan was first to react. "One Irish Car Bomb, and a Killian's in a bottle."

"And for you?" He asked Lynnie.

"Uh…no car bombing for me, I'll have a Buttery Nipple and a Bud Light."

"Coming right up!"

"What's with the drink order, missy?" Lynnie

160

questioned her friend.

"Well, we *are* in an Irish Pub, so I figured I'd have a shot or two. Besides, I love those and the only time I drink shots is when I'm pissed, sad, or with you."

"Yeah true, but it's usually Patron."

"Those are my sad and pissed off nights."

"Well then…"

The Lad returned with all of the drinks and shots.

"You know…he kind of looks Irish."

"I guess so." Logan barely agreed.

"Speaking of Irish…"

"I'm Scottish you dip shit." Logan's eyebrows furled together then, she smiled.

"I know that…I was about to tell you about this new girl that I met when I was in Chicago on the last leg of the tour."

"Oh…" With a quick bat of the eyes and her best *I'm sorry* look, Logan smiled.

"Anyway, there was a girl in the bar that was from Ireland. She's was born here but lived most of her life over there. She had blonde hair with a reddish tint, light colored eyes and skin, and she was complete with the Irish tongue rolling accent."

"Interesting, did you hook up with her?"

"Didn't you grow up in Scotland?" Lynnie changed the subject.

"I only spent the summers in Scotland with my Grandparents as a child, up until I was a teenager."

"I've always wanted to go to another country. I wouldn't know which one to go to though, there are so many."

"I've been to many of them. Although, I haven't been back to Scotland since my Grandparents passed away a few years ago. I guess I just don't have the time anymore."

"Do you keep in touch with your family there?"

"Yeah, I have Aunts, Uncles, and Cousins that live over there. My mother and father were the only ones in their families to move to the states. I would've been born in Scotland if they had waited a year. My Grandparents use to say 'Reid Greer turned against his Clan to have relations with Amelee Rodderick. We pity him.' My grandparents chastised my father for not only marrying a woman from the family that they were at war with, but then he cowardly moved to the States to bore his only child, and then join the Military after he became a citizen. Boy, did that piss them off!"

"Logan this is the most I've heard you talk about your family since I've known you, and I've known you for years!"

"Haha, I guess I just thought of it out of the blue." She shrugged with a smile.

"So why were they at war?"

"Land."

"How stupid."

"True, but a over hundred years ago land was all people had. The families were already fighting way before my Grandparents ever even met each other. And it still continues to this day."

"Wow, that's ridiculous."

"Yeah, when I was a kid I'd spend the summers with my Greer Grandparents and then see my Rodderick Grandparents just before I came back. I guess you can say I learned most of my family heritage from the Greer's. I turned out okay though."

"I'd say you did. So I guess not many people

know about your heritage."

"No, I don't talk about it much."

The bartender appeared with a complete second round for the ladies as Lynnie began telling the tale of her family, which wasn't much except for the fact the she was from a small poor family in Georgia and was raised by the black folks around town. That's where she learned to play the blues and the slide guitar the way she does.

"Hey so you never told me whether or not you hooked up with the lassie?"

"Oh...yeah I spent some time with her while I was there." Lynnie smiled.

"Will you ever see her again?"

"I doubt it, but I am playing there again in two months and she has my webpage and email so she'll know when I'm back."

"That's good."

"Speaking of...well not really hooking up...but did you get to see Chaney while you were in L.A.?"

"Yeah, I always try to see her. She's doing really well. I'm happy for her."

"Miss her?"

"All the time, she's my best friend and I miss that part. I'll always love her, but we fell out of love a long time ago."

"I watch her show on TV sometimes when I catch it on."

"I was able to see a live production of it not long ago. She's funnier now than she ever was. I laughed my ass off."

"Do you think you'll ever marry again?"

The bartender was right on schedule with their third round.

"Well…" Lynnie waited for a response.

"I dunno…I, never say never, but I can't seem to find anyone worth dating much less giving my life to them." Logan wondered where that question came from.

"Hell I hear ya."

"I guess if the right woman came along…"

"Here's to the right woman coming through that door." They clanked glasses. In the back of her mind Logan toasted that Brooke's marriage fail from one end to the other. She grinned sheepishly.

***

When they finally left the bar Logan was happy she lived close by since she wasn't much of a good 'drunk driver'. Lynnie followed her and slept in the spare room. She was up early and shared a pot of coffee with Logan before she left. Logan spent the rest of the day nursing a hang over and cleaning the inches of dust off of everything in her condo since she fired her latest housekeeper for trying to steal a plastic plant. Logan still didn't quite get that one.

***

Monday arrived all too quickly as the lean, nude, tanned figure slipped out of the satin sheets to turn the ringing alarm clock off. *Wake up Greer, another day…another couple of dollars after all of the overtime off the clock and Uncle Sam's fat ass cut.* She jumped in the steamy hot shower, wishing for another hour of dreamless sleep.

164

Fate Vs. Destiny

***

Logan was sitting at her desk when her cell phone rang.

"Greer."

"Agent Greer, this is Walter Hudson."

"Hi."

"How far are you with your hydraulic research?"

"My flight leaves for Seattle in an hour. I'm meeting with Boeing today to discuss their input and then I'm staying overnight. Tomorrow I'm flying to D.C. to meet with Airbus at their North American Headquarters."

"Will you be able to get the information that you're looking for there?"

"If not I'll be flying to Toulouse, France. That's where Airbus is actually located."

"I know, I hope you find it here. That's a long flight and jet lag from hell."

"Yes Sir, that much I know."

"You don't have to stop in the office tomorrow, just call and let me know where you stand with this. We should be looking at about six months or so until we can go in front of the board with the proposed regulation."

"Yes Sir.

Eleven

The winter months and Holidays slowly rolled by with no incidents. Logan spent most of her time between the bar, the gym, and running on the beach every second that she wasn't behind her desk staring at reports, signing papers, and listening to conference calls. She had traveled back and forth across the country over four months, going to meetings with different aircraft engineers trying to put together research information on one of the safety regulations.

***

"Damn it Arnold, I told you I needed that report yesterday. I'm leaving in the morning for D.C. and I can't take this to the FAA without having the Boeing report on my desk." Logan paced in front of the window in her charcoal gray Armani suit yelling at the speaker phone on the desk. *Come on you pencil dick piece of shit. Don't ruin this for me I've spent three months trying to get this safety regulation passed and I'll be damned if some intern is going to fuck this up for me.*

"Yes Ma'am, Agent Greer. I'll let you know as soon as I find it. I'm very sorry that I lost it, I thought I had already faxed it to you."

Fate Vs. Destiny

"Well news flash! You didn't fax it to me!"

"Yes Ma'am."

She slammed the phone to hang it up. "Goddamn it! What the hell am I going to do without this report? My research is shot to hell. I swear I'll fly out to Seattle and kill that pencil dick intern myself if he doesn't find this."

Logan couldn't stand the pacing anymore and decided to go walk the concourse and watch the flights take off. She stopped at the secretary's desk on the way out of the office.

"If I receive a fax, any fax, at all, call my cell. I'll be in the concourse or on the tarmac."

"Yes Ma'am."

***

Three hours had gone by and Logan was now finishing up the documentation for her meeting in the morning. As she was about to call Boeing for the fifth time, the fax machine beeped and started spitting out papers. Logan grabbed the stack and saw *Boeing* printed across the top. *Oh thank god!* She grabbed the stack and tossed it neatly into her briefcase.

Logan went for a short run as the sun went down. She stopped halfway to her destination and sat in the sand to watch the tide go back out. *I've talked to you on the phone and that took me a while to get use to, but luckily for me, I haven't seen you in six months. Thanks to my rearranging my meetings in D.C., now I have to not only talk to you in person, but you'll be in the room as part of the Aeronautical Safety Commission that votes on this new regulation that I'm purposing. You could blow this for me, not that I think you would.* "Be strong Logan,

167

push everything away. You've been working on this for over a year now and you've come further than ever before in the last six months. You have this in the bag. Don't worry about her. She's another notch in your belt and another body in a chair at that table as far as your concerned."

She got back up and started running back towards her Condo building under the stars. Once inside she stopped in the gym and laced up her gloves. The butterflies in her stomach were going crazy from having to see Brooke again. *I don't care to see you at all damn it*...The punches started as she smacked the black leather bag. *Left...right...left, right, left...right, right...left, right...left. You can get through this Greer, just treat her like a colleague...left, right...right, left, right...left.* The sweat rolled off her brow.

***

Nine o'clock a.m., Logan walked into the NTSB Headquarters building. Walter Hudson met her when she exited the elevator.

"Good Morning, Agent Greer."

"Agent Hudson." She nodded.

Logan didn't have to turn around, she smelled the familiar aroma of flowers and soap before she ever heard the sweet sounding voice. *Here we go!*

"Agent Greer. Good to see you again."

"Miss McCabe or is it Taglia now?" Logan asked out of politeness.

"McCabe." Brooke turned away quickly.

***

Everyone went into the conference room together. Logan was speaking to Walter so she was one of the last to enter and in turn she was stuck sitting next to Brooke. Walter stood up and began the meeting. He started the quarterly meeting as usual, with the latest Accident reports minor to major, knocking on wood that they hadn't had a major accident in eight months. Then, he moved on to safety regulations just before he introduced Logan and invited her to the podium.

"Good Morning everyone, you all know me by now, my name is Logan Greer. I'm up here this morning to introduce a new safety regulation to all of you and hopefully have it voted into commission." She stopped to pass out thick report packets to everyone at the large oval table. "Now this is a feature that I believe as well as Boeing, will stop a lot of the hydraulic problems that we've been having with the GE 3267 Turbine Jet Engine. This engine is found on most of the 727 and 737 model planes. This particular regulation will force General Electric and other similar sized engine manufacturers to separate their hydraulic systems creating a dual or tri-flowing circuit instead of a single circuit. This means if the hydro system blows a line on one engine it will be contained to that engine and able to be shut down singly. As you are all aware at the present time, if there is a hydro system problem the planes try to land as soon as possible, but in some instances they have had to shut the system down. In turn, both or all three of the engines shut down simultaneously because of the single circuit and this has caused many accidents. We all know a 727 or a 737 is perfectly capable of continuing a safe flight on a single engine, therefore it is in our best interest to allow this regulation and move to begin remodeling the system on the entire fleet of 727 and 737 series airplanes. Are there any questions?"

"How costly is this remodel?" One of the FAA Safety team members spoke first.

"I've spoken to Boeing and Airbus. Right now, Airbus is currently not using this engine. Boeing has told me that it should be estimated at a thousand dollars worth of parts per engine and approximately fifteen hours per engine."

"That's a hefty chunk of dollars and time, Agent Greer." Brooke had a point.

"Yes you're correct, but a few thousand dollars per plane is worth it when it comes to over five-hundred lives that we've lost due to this problem." Logan shot back.

A few others debated her theories for over an hour, then Walter Hudson stood up and took the podium. "I'll ask all of you to now vote whether or not you agree with this proposal and are willing to commission this regulation with your signature."

***

Thirty minutes went by as everyone slowly went into the booth to vote. Logan paced the floor around the corner.

"You're going to wear a path in the tile."

Logan could smell her from a mile away. "I'm fine." She growled.

"I didn't ask."

"You implied."

"Ladies and Gentlemen the votes are tallied.

Please regroup in the conference room." Walter had a stout voice that didn't match his appearance at all.

"I'm pleased to announce that with a twenty-nine to one gain, Safety Regulation number G0756 has been commissioned to the NTSB and FAA Aeronautical Safety Regulations. Remodels on the aircrafts will be mandatory, immediately following the regulation update to all 727 and 737 air carriers."

Logan clinched her fist under the table to keep from screaming with excitement. She didn't notice Brooke grab her hand briefly.

"Thank you Agent Greer for bringing this new advancement to our attention. And again safe flying, this meeting is now adjourned."

Walter Hudson walked out of the meeting room with Logan. "Agent Greer, I'm very pleased with your enthusiasm and hard work. It has definitely paid off with this regulation being passed. I couldn't ask for a more thorough and professional IIC and Safety Committee Board Member on my team. You'll make an excellent department head one day. Believe it or not, this entire building looks up to you in one way or another."

"Thank you Sir." Logan shook his hand and headed towards the elevator.

***

Outside of the building, Logan was hailing a cab when she smelled the familiar scent lingering. *Damn her!*

"Wait before you take off."

"Why should I? We discussed everything in the meeting. Read your report if you have anymore questions email me or call me at my office."

"Have dinner with me."

Logan turned to face her. "Excuse me?"

"You heard me, have dinner with me, Logan."

"What the hell is wrong with you? No!"

"Please, at least have a drink with me before you fly out of my life for another six months."

"That's your problem not mine."

"Logan, please…all I'm asking is for you to have a conversation with me."

Logan slammed the cab door and sent him on his way.

"Where's your husband?"

"We're not married." Brooke said flatly.

"Okay…where's your fiancé?"

"I left him two months ago."

"Huh…"

"Dinner…a drink…that's all I'm asking, Logan, an hour of your time."

"I don't care to hear the sob story of your life, Brooke. I've moved on incase you haven't noticed."

"I know you have. I…I just want to talk to you."

"You're not going to leave me alone until I do are you?"

"No, you know how persistent I am." She smiled wryly.

Logan remembered back to how they first got started. "I know."

"One more hour with me won't kill you, Logan. I didn't realize you hated me this much."

"Hate is a strong word Brooke, equally as strong as Love. It's very hard to Love someone and Hate them too."

"I see...an hour?"

Fate Vs. Destiny
"Fine…where are we going?"

***

An hour later Logan had learned how Brooke did a large amount of soul searching and she discovered that she really wasn't happy with Matthew and severely missed Logan. The companionship and the unannounced love between them was the hardest thing she ever had to let go of. She explained to Logan how she couldn't deal with it any longer and she finally told Matthew the truth and they split and went through counseling at first. A month later she completely ended it and has been on her own for two months now trying to get her life back in order. She continued counseling on her own to try and figure out her life.

Logan listened, but never offered a condolence or word of advice. She did tell Brooke that all she ever wanted was for her to be happy, and as long as she could look her in the eyes and tell her she was honestly happy, then it didn't matter who she was with. On that note, she paid the bar tab, grabbed Brooke's hand, leaned over and kissed her cheek, and left the bar.

***

Logan caught a late flight back home. She was strong enough to fight off the tears until she walked into her Condo. The warm droplets were flowing down her cheeks before she could get out of her business suit. *Damn you. Brooke, I let you get right to me…again!* She quickly dried her face and jumped in the steamy hot shower. *How can I love you so much after everything you*

173

did to me? I can't just let you waltz right back into my life. I deserve happiness goddamn it!

***

The next day went by slowly. Logan listened to three conference calls and met with a few of the air carriers about the new regulation before she headed home, finally ending her week. Yesterday had been the clincher to *Hell week*.

Logan walked through the doors of her Condo lobby and Brooke was sitting on one of the chairs. Logan blinked a few times and opened her eyes again. Brooke was walking towards her. *What now?*

"I wasn't finished yesterday. You left before I could tell you...before I could..."

"Spill it, Brooke. What is so important that you flew all the way dow..."

"I love you Logan, I've been in love with you for a long time." A tear rolled down Brooke's face.

Logan didn't know what to say. Of course she wanted to say it back, but how could she, after everything that had happened? She was completely speechless. The last time they said those words everything was turned upside down.

"Say something, Logan."

"Damn you, how can you come here and do this to me? Do you ever stop?"

"What?" Brooke was confused.

"You broke my fucking heart, Brooke. Then you smiled and threw your arms around him. What am I suppose to say?"

"I'm sorry, Logan. I never meant to hurt you. I

guess I had to find myself and it took me almost ruining my life to realize how much I wanted to be with you and I didn't…don't care who knows it. I want you in my life, you're all I want, Logan. I love you so much."

Logan felt a tear escape her eye. She lowered her head trying not to show Brooke her face. She knew Brooke could read her eyes like a book.

"I…I just don't…Brooke, I don't know if I can go though this again. I'm not strong enough to let go of you twice."

"I'm never going to hurt you again, Logan. I don't ever want to be without you again. I love you."

God help me. "I love you too. I can't stop, no matter how hard I try." Logan reached over and pulled Brooke into her arms. She held her warm body against her for what seemed like minutes. Then she bent her head slightly and pressed her lips to the smaller woman. Their lips met softly, then, progressed fiercely as their tongues explored deeper. Logan picked Brooke up against her, unaware that were standing in the lobby of her Condo building.

"I want you so bad, Logan…" Brooke broke the kiss long enough to speak through ragged breaths. "But …we…we shou…uh…" She finally blurted out. "We're standing in the lobby!"

Logan slowly looked past Brooke and noticed the few people watching them. *Opps.* She let Brooke go as she bent down to retrieve her briefcase.

As soon as the elevator doors closed Brooke pushed Logan against the back wall. She grabbed a handful of Logan's short blond hair and pulled the slightly taller woman down into an erotically charged kiss, sucking her tongue and biting her lips. Logan put both palms flat against Brooke's firm butt and squeezed, pulling the petite woman tightly against her. The passionate kissing and fondling continued until the elevator started to move back down. The open door on the Penthouse floor had gone unnoticed by the woman and the elevator was now heading back to the ground floor.

"Damn it!" Logan rushed to the button panel and immediately put her codes in to go back up to the Penthouse floor. As the elevator started to ascend once more both woman shook their heads and laughed.

They finally made it into Logan's Condo. Brooke took in the modern, contemporary design with the breath taking ocean front view. "I remember this place being exceptionally perfect, just like you." She smiled.

Logan blushed, just barely, but Brooke knew it. The tops of Logan's ears always turned red when she was blushing. In fact, that was the only sign that would give it away. "Would you like a drink?" Logan asked, trying to change the subject of her bloodshot ears.

"Nah." Brooke walked up to her, stood on the tips of her toes and kissed one crimson colored ear. "You're so damn cute!"

"Cute huh! I'll show you cute!" Logan picked Brooke up and set her on top of the counter next to the stove. Their lips met softly. Brooke's mouth opened, inviting Logan to probe further. The kiss became unmanageable as Brooke began to rid Logan of her suit jacket then unbuttoned her blouse. Logan's hands wandered underneath the back of Brooke's silk top, then down to the zipper on her skirt. She stopped long enough to remove her gun and its holster. She set them both on the kitchen counter.

176

Fate Vs. Destiny

Minutes later both women were completely topless. Brooke had a death grip on Logan's waist with her legs as Logan again picked her up. She walked around the corner towards her bedroom and laid the most beautiful woman she had ever met onto her bed. Since Brooke had already kicked her heels off in the kitchen, Logan slipped out of her shoes and climbed up next to her. Brooke quickly climbed on top of Logan and bent her head to tease her with a flick of her tongue against soft lips as her long honey colored hair fell down around Logan's face. A faint moan escaped Logan's mouth. Brooke stopped long enough to gaze into gorgeous moonlit bluish-green eyes. "You still have clothes on."

"Yeah, so do you."

"Hmm..." Brooke moved to the side and slid Logan's pants and panties off. "Don't worry. I won't wrinkle your Armani pants." She laughed.

"I'm not worried about my pants."

"Aw, then why the sad look all of a sudden?"

"You're still half dressed." Logan smirked, as she rolled Brooke onto her back and slipped the skirt off to reveal a lace thong underneath. "Mm...you're so beautiful Brooke."

Brooke smiled shyly. "Come here."

Logan straddled Brooke's bare thigh and slid down slowly.

"Ah...it feels so good when you do that."

Logan again slid herself along the silky smooth skin. Brooke could feel Logan's wetness coat her leg. Logan stayed against Brooke's leg, their lips met passionately once more as their tongues slow danced together. Logan gradually moved her hand from Brooke's breasts, across her tan abdomen, down one thigh and back to the tiny patch of silky hair in the center. She nonchalantly ran her fingers delicately through the moist folds of skin as she continued breathlessly kissing Brooke. Unable to withstand the teasing any longer, Brooke reached down and grabbed Logan's hand. "Go inside me..."

Logan was immediately lost in all of the wetness as two fingers slid easily inside of Brooke. She felt the muscles tense around her, then, release to let her penetrate deeper and harder. Brooke grabbed Logan's hair and pulled her into a tight embrace. She ran her nails mildly up Logan's back, careful not to hurt her. Logan continued soft gentle kisses along Brooke's ears and neck, meticulously stopping to taste her mouth. She concentrated on the rapid heartbeat and unfathomed breathing of the woman in her arms. Brooke ran her hand down Logan's side and around her thigh. She stopped to adjust so that she could get between Logan's thighs. She gracefully slid two fingers through the warm liquid, smooth muscles tightened against her as Logan let out a deep breath against her neck, ending with a tiny moan. They moved together in perfect rhythm thrusting in and out of each other, gradually moving towards the climax they were waiting so desperately for. Logan tauntingly bit Brooke's bottom lip as she parted her mouth for a deep, lustful kiss. Midway through the kiss, their bodies were on fire. They looked into each others eyes and held each other tightly as ecstasy passed between them and filled the room. When their heartbeats finally slowed they shared a warm, gentle kiss.

"I love you, Logan."

Logan closed her eyes briefly. *Thank you.* Then, she opened them to see this beautiful angel lying in her arms. "I love you too, Brooke."

***

Three hours later Brooke awoke to a cold, empty bed. She sauntered over to the open French doors, leading to the balcony. Logan was leaning against the rail wearing a short, dark green terry-cloth robe. She had woken up shortly after falling asleep, laid there and watched Brooke sleep in her arms for an hour, then stood there gazing out at the sea and the stars for another hour.

"I caught you." Brooke walked up and wrapped her arms around the slightly taller woman.

"Come here, you're naked." Logan turned and opened her robe. She pulled Brooke against her and wrapped the flaps of the robe around them. "And yes, I guess you did catch me. I have a hard time sleeping, especially when my head is spinning a hundred miles an hour."

"Aw…what's wrong honey?"

Logan took a deep breath and exhaled slowly. "I'm scared and confused. I don't know if I can do this Brooke."

"What do you mean?"

"I…I guess…" She took another deep breath. "I don't trust you."

"What! Logan, what the hell are you talking about? You're scaring me." Brooke tried to back away but Logan held her tightly.

"Please listen to me, don't just hear me. This is all happening so fast, you, here, in my bed. I'm not ready for this. I've been beside myself trying so hard to let you go. Now this…I mean…what happens if you decide to go

179

back to him?"

"Logan I would never do that…"

"Brooke, never say never. Look at everything that we've gone through this past year and a half. You weren't exactly honest with me."

"You will never let me live that down will you?"

"I can't just forget how you tore my heart out of my chest and stomped on it like you didn't care."

"I did care…Logan I was in love with you and with him at the same time. What the hell was I suppose to do?"

"Be honest with me. That's all I ever asked of you."

"I'm trying to start over…with you…a new life with you, Logan…"

"I'm not sure if that's what I want…I mean…"

"You just made love to me like it was what you wanted. What's changed?"

"Nothing's changed. I've been in love with you for a very long time. I just can't get hurt anymore, Brooke, especially by you."

"I'm sorry for hurting you. I never meant to. I don't ever want to hurt you again."

"I'm sure you didn't want to in the first place, but it happened. This happened. Brooke, life happens."

"What are you saying? I'm confused."

"I'm saying what happens when having a life with me isn't good enough for Brooke anymore? It would kill me to have you finally, and then have you destroy me by leaving me."

"I'm not going anywhere, honey. I love you. I'm here with you right now."

"I love you too, but what happens tomorrow or

the day after that when you go *home*?"

"I…uh…I haven't thought about that. I'm not like you, Logan. I live in the now, not the future."

Logan was silent. A lonely tear ran down her cheek. She was happy the darkness outside hid the truth from the woman in her arms.

"I guess I could put in for a transfer and move down here or you could finally move to D.C., where you *should* be working anyway."

"Marry me." Logan said flatly.

"I'm sure I'd get the transfer to JIA, we don't have…WHAT!?" Brooke's eyes were bugging out of her head.

"Marry me, Brooke."

"Uh…" Brooke stepped back out of the robe and looked up into bluish-green eyes staring back at her. "Logan!"

"I'm serious." Logan stood her ground, her heart was about to erupt from the pressure flowing through her mind.

"Uh…we…uh…I…" Brooke swore she couldn't breath. The words just wouldn't come out. "Uh…We never even dated!"

Logan grabbed Brooke's hands and held them against her frantically beating chest. "I love you and I'm serious. Brooke McCabe, will you marry me?" *Please hold me up legs, I can't afford embarrassment now!* She could feel her legs shaking and her knees about to buckle.

Brooke was praying that she didn't faint. Still speechless, she tried once more to speak. "Ye...uh…I…" She desperately tried to pull herself together. Finally, reality sank in as a tear slid down her check. "Yes, Logan, yes I'll marry you."

Logan picked the smaller woman up against her in a warm embrace under the stars. Their lips met with passionate desire, tongues burning to be against each other. Their naked bodies were pressed together as the kiss ended slowly.

"I love you so much." Logan held Brooke tightly.

"I love you too, more than I ever thought possible...Logan..."

"Yes..."

"Make love to me until the sun comes up."

Logan walked her backwards through the open doors straight to the bed.

Twelve

After another long lovemaking session ended, they fell asleep tangled around each other and wrapped up in the sheets. Hours later, both women awoke and showered together, carelessly using all of the hot water as they explored each others body once more.

"I left my suitcase in the rental car. I need to borrow some clothes so I can run down and get it." Brooke popped her head into the kitchen where Logan was amidst rustling pots and pans. She looked up at the naked figure.

"I think you should go down there like that." She stated nonchalantly.

"Okay, if that's what you want." Brooke walked through the foyer towards the door. Logan jumped and ran after her.

"I was only kidding!"

"I know, I just wanted to see the look on your face when I opened that door." Brooke smiled from ear to ear.

"You're so damn adorable. Come here!" Logan swept Brooke up into her arms and kissed her forehead.

"So Chef Greer, what's on the brunch menu?"

"Uh...hmm...I'm not sure."

"Oh, is that a fact? By the sounds coming from the cabinets I was going to ask if you had ever cooked before."

"Hey, that's not funny. I cook! Just not often, so I'm a bit nervous."

"Would you like me to cook?"

"NO! ...I mean this is my house and you're my guest and I want to cook for you."

"Uh huh, I see. That dinner you made for me was amazing the last time I was here. Anyway, I'll go put on some clothes so I can go get my suitcase and I'll leave you to it." Brooke kissed Logan's lips and lingered just long enough to feel her lips part for a deeper kiss and her hips thrust against her.

"Tease!" Logan sneered as she went back to the kitchen. *What the hell am I going to make?*

***

After they finished their meal, consisting of a bacon, egg, and cheese croissant for Brooke and a bacon and cheese croissant for Logan, both women sat out on the balcony sipping coffee and watching the tide roll in on the beach.

"So I guess we have a lot to talk about."

"We do?" Logan questioned.

"I do believe you proposed and if I do recall correctly, I said yes."

"Is that so?" Logan smiled. "Where do we begin?"

"How about, who's moving? How long do you want to be engaged? When's a good time for a ceremony? Where would we have it? Who would be there? Do you have a big family? When will I meet them? Will they be there? What will we tell our jobs? Do you want a..."

Fate Vs. Destiny

"Whoa…slow down Brooke."

"I'm sorry, I'm nervous and excited."

"I am too, but the horse is galloping at full speed and I'm barely in the saddle. We should start with one thing at a time. I know our jobs are the most important."

"That's also the hardest. I mean I don't know about the NTSB, but the FAA is so goddamn right wing it's ridiculous."

"Yeah, the NTSB too, it's because of our asshole President and his religious views."

"What do you think they'll do?"

"I really doubt the Government is going to fire two of their best employees because they're lesbians who happen to be marrying each other."

"I don't think they will either, but you never know."

"It would be the biggest lawsuit against the government and the Press would eat it up and spit it all over the Whitehouse lawn. Don't worry about it, we won't lose our jobs. The major question is, are you prepared to move?"

"Me? Why me?"

"I lived in D.C. for the first two years and I hated it. I like it down here. I really enjoy working out of JIA. I deal with less bullshit than when I was up there."

"It's not easy for me to just transfer. I work out of the FAA Main Building. Besides, I don't like having neighbors on the other side of the walls."

Logan rolled her eyes. "Fine, I can compromise if you can. You put in for a transfer to work out of JIA and I'll sell my Condo so we can buy a house together."

"Hmm…"

"Brooke we don't have to do this Monday

185

morning. We can wait and think it through before we make some drastic change that will effect both of our lives forever."

"We made that change last night when we decided to get married, Logan. I don't want to live in D.C. and you live in Jacksonville, we'd never see each other."

"I know what you're saying. We should probably do it though."

"What? You live here and me up there?"

"Yeah, only until we decide what's best."

"What's best? What do you mean? You're not second guessing this, are you Logan?"

Logan grabbed Brooke's hand and held it tightly. "No, of course not, I love you. I want to be right next to you for the rest of my life. All I'm saying is we should wait until you get a transfer and we find a house to buy."

"What if I get an okay quickly and have to move down?"

"Then you can move into the Condo with me until it's sold and we buy a house. I don't know how the FAA works, but the NTSB took me six months to get my okay to relocate."

"That's a long time!"

"Not really when you think about it. I flew down and found a place to buy. Then, I flew back to D.C. and started slowly packing up my apartment. A month later I made an offer on the Condo and bought it a month after that. I flew down on the weekends to supervise the remodeling crew that was here painting and putting in new carpet and tile. After that I started moving stuff down, little this week, a little that week. One day my transfer paperwork came across my desk and I had to report to JIA for work the following Monday, assholes gave me three days to find a place and move. Luckily, I was practically finished. I packed up my truck with what was left and here I am."

"Cute story, but what's with you and having neighbors up your ass?"

"Huh?"

"Apartment, Condo, what's next?"

"A house."

They both laughed.

"I do love the view here though."

"I'm not moving off of the beach, just so you know. Our house will have to be oceanfront."

"Compromise honey...I want a dog."

"What!"

Brooke smiled. "You heard me. I want a dog."

"We'll never be home and then when we're out on an investigation who will watch Fido?"

"Fido? I'll be damned if my dog's name will be Fido! Besides, I'm sure we will have friends that he or she can stay with."

"For three months?"

"I see your point; we can discuss it at a later time."

"Thank you." Logan smiled and kissed the top of Brooke's hand.

***

Two weeks later Logan was sitting at her desk signing paperwork and reading documents on her computer. "I swear I sign more papers and read more bullshit than I ever thought possible." Just as she was about to download the latest email attachment, her cell phone rang the familiar Waltz tune.

"Agent Greer."

"Hey, sweetness." Brooke spoke softly.

"Hello, yourself." Logan's heart skipped a beat and she smiled.

"How's your day going?" Brooke asked.

"Shitty, but typical, I'm up to my elbows in paperwork and email."

"Yeah, me too."

"So I was thinking…"

"Uh huh…"

"How about September?"

"September? For what?" Logan questioned.

"Our wedding…silly." Brooke laughed.

"What?" Logan almost dropped the phone.

"We should start thinking about a date."

We've been engaged for two weeks! Logan's mind raced. "Sweetheart, that's four months away."

"I know, but that's a good month with work."

"You do have a point there, I'm usually finished with my inspections towards the end of July and I don't go back out again until January."

"My schedule runs a little different. I don't do as much as you do. Most of my work is on the computer and over the phone. I only inspect once a year and that's usually January."

"How long does it take you?"

"A month usually, sometimes less if I don't run into any problems. Basically I make sure all of the Airlines have the new regulations and the updates for the upcoming year by November. Then I spend the month of January making sure these are in place and everything else is still being followed according to protocol. When all is well, I go home."

Logan sat back in her chair. "Must be nice, I do that every month. No wonder I spend two to three months cleaning up bullshit in the field."

"Must we really argue about our jobs?"

"No. I'm just stating facts."

"I see, well state some facts about our wedding and what date you think is good for you so we can start planning."

"You just put in for your transfer yesterday."

"Yeah…"

"Why are you so eager?"

"I'm in love with you; forgive me if I want to be down there by your side as your wife!"

Ouch! Damn it, Greer. "I'm sorry, I love you too and I can't wait to be married to you. It's just happening so fast."

"I know, our jobs are just so damn demanding."

"It's going to be hard to invite a bunch of people and everything, what if we get a call?"

"Yeah, I thought about that too. Honestly, I'd like you to meet my Mom and Dad and a few close friends first. But, I really want to get married on a beach somewhere, just you and me."

"I like that idea…I like that idea a lot. I've been through a large formal wedding and I don't need to do it again. My parents live here in the States, but the rest of my family is in Scotland so they won't make it anyway. How does Hawaii sound?" Logan opened the Calendar on her computer and searched the month of September.

"Great!"

"The tenth looks good for me."

"Um…let me see." Brooke paused to check her

Calendar. "Yeah, the tenth sounds fine."

"It's set then. We can clear our schedules for two weeks and fly out a couple days in advance to do the last minute arrangements, get married, then, spend the rest of the time on our honeymoon there. Unless, you want to go somewhere else?"

"No, that sounds nice, I like it there."

"Good." Logan smiled through the phone. "I wish I could hold you and kiss you right now."

"Me too! I miss your skin." Brooke spoke softly.

"Mm…I miss all of you!"

"You do know we'll both be on call."

"Yeah, knock on wood all of the birds stay in the air during those two weeks."

"No shit! Oh I would be so pissed!" Logan spat out then quickly changed the subject. "Sweetheart?"

"Yes…"

"What time are you coming to me tonight?"

Brooke's heart began to race. "My flight leaves in an hour."

"I'll be the blond at the gate." Logan stated.

"Oh yeah? The hot one? I like her!"

"You bet." Logan closed her phone and sat back in her desk chair. *My god, she makes me giddy like a little kid!*

***

Logan opened her phone back up and smashed speed dial button number one.

"NTSB Aviation Headquarters, this is Walter Hudson."

"Hey, this is Agent Greer…"

"How's it going Logan?"

"Not bad, I'm calling because I need to give notice for personal time out of the office. I realize I'll still be on call of course. But, from September eighth thru the twenty fifth I won't be here."

"Vacation?"

"I'm getting married…in Hawaii."

"Oh." The man's voice sounded a little shocked. "I had no idea...congratulations."

"Thanks."

***

Another week went by. Logan sat at her desk, took a deep breath, held it for as long as she could, then dialed a number on her cell phone.

"Hello?"

"Chaney, its Logan."

"Hey! How are you?"

"Good…you?"

"I've been told I'm great, but you already know that." Chaney smirked.

Logan laughed. "Yeah, yeah, yeah."

"So, what do I owe the pleasure of a mid morning Wednesday phone call? Are you in town…did something crash?"

Logan laughed once more. Chaney always liked to hear her laugh. At least she knew Logan was okay when she was laughing.

"No nothing crashed. I'm sitting in my office at JIA."

"Oh. You sound like you're in a really good mood."

"I am, I wanted to do this in person, but my schedule is so hectic right now there is no way that I could come out there."

"It sounds serious, are you okay?"

"Yeah, I'm just nervous."

"About?" Chaney questioned.

Logan took another deep breath and turned to look out at the runway.

"Logan?" Chaney's voice took a serious tone.

"I'm getting married…"

"You're what?!" Logan's ex-wife almost dropped the phone.

"I'm getting married…"

"Oh my god...what...to who...when?"

"Brooke McCabe."

"Not the girl that broke your heart." Chaney said wryly.

"Long story short, I guess things worked themselves out."

"Why marriage?"

"We're in love."

"Wow, I mean I'm happy for you…this is just a little much."

"I know…I'm sorry, I wanted to tell you face to face."

"I understand. It's funny how reality sets in three years later."

"Yeah, the night we got engaged I thought about you and how all of that happened for us. I cried for a minute then all of a sudden the tears stopped and I was happy, happier than I've been in a long time. I love her so much."

"I'm glad things worked out for you. You deserve

it Logan."

"Thank you, that means a lot coming from you."

"You're welcome. So when's the big day?"

"September tenth. We're flying to Hawaii and doing it there, just the two of us. It's easier that way, because we'll both be on call to the government if there's a crash."

"Will I get to meet her eventually? You know I need to approve of her." Chaney laughed.

"Of course you will, next time I go to Cali."

"You've seen her on TV with me right?"

"Uh…yeah I think so, isn't she short and petite with long hair."

Logan laughed. "Yeah. That's her. She's a few inches shorter than me and built a little smaller."

"I didn't see her up close but she looks pretty on TV, then again the news woman is hot on TV and she's ugly as hell in person."

"Oh no." Logan chuckled. "She's beautiful in person and on TV. Trust me, I thought you were beautiful, still do."

"Touché."

Logan hung up and dialed again.

"Lynnie?"

"Hey Logan, What's up?"

"I'm uh…getting married."

"You're what?! Excuse me!" Lynnie shouted into the phone.

"Getting married."

"To who? When? What the hell?" Lynnie was still shouting.

"Her name is Brooke, she's also a government agent, but for the FAA. We're getting married in Hawaii

September tenth. I'm sorry I never really told you about her. It's a very long story. We've been off and on for a long time and we love each other a lot."

"Wow. I knew something was up, you've been acting weird for the past few months."

"Yeah, I wanted to tell you, I guess I just bottled it up for a long time. We've had a rocky year and a half…"

"Year and a half? What the hell?" Lynnie shouted again.

"It's a long story. Hey wanna meet for a drink tonight? I'll tell you the whole story so you can stop shouting at me."

"This I wouldn't miss! What time?"

"The Irish pub by my house at eight."

"Sounds good…oh and by the way, why Hawaii? Do you not want your only friend to go?"

Logan laughed. "I'll explain that too!"

***

Lynnie could barely swallow her beer as Logan sat there explaining the past year and a half to her.

"Oh my god, I had no idea. I mean I know you were acting weird, but hell you always act weird." She snickered. "So what does she look like?"

"Oh yeah, sorry, she's a few inches shorter than me and built a little bit smaller, she's fairly tiny. She has long honey colored hair that goes almost to her butt, olive colored skin, and tantalizing green eyes that have a slight blue tint in the sun."

"She sounds beautiful."

Logan smiled. "She is. You'll meet her soon, I

194

promise. I'm going up North to visit her and meet her parents next month."

"Do they know?"

"Yeah, they're not happy about it, but they're willing to meet me and go from there."

"Ouch!"

"Tell me about it."

"Does Chaney know?"

"Yeah."

Thirteen

Logan's visit with Brooke's parents went over like a bull in a china shop in the beginning. By the end of the weekend they were all getting along, finally having pleasant conversations. Logan could tell they weren't jumping for joy to see their daughter as a 'lesbian', but they enjoyed seeing her happy and in love.

Logan stepped on the plane to head back home. *Glad that's over. The in-laws retracted their horns and fangs by Sunday. Maybe it's because they're religious. Hmm...who the hell knows? All I know is they are getting along with me for the sake of their baby girl who is going to be my wife in eight weeks...Holy shit! EIGHT WEEKS!!!!!*

"Ma'am...excuse me miss? Would you like a drink?" The flight attendant startled Logan.

"Uh...yes! Make it the stiffest thing you have on board please...straight up on the rocks."

"Yes Ma'am."

Eight weeks! Get a grip, Greer, you started this, you love that woman more than life, it'll be a piece of cake...wedding cake. She giggled to herself.

***

Two weeks later Brooke moved in with Logan. Disorder took over the Condo as Brooke added some of her things to the living room and bedroom; most of her belongings went in storage.

"Are we ever going to find a house that we agree on?" Brooke asked wryly.

"I'm sure we will, give it time."

"Time, your Condo is practically sold Logan. We're on borrowed time until it goes to closing."

Logan nodded her head in agreement. "Hey, after dinner I need to run an errand, will you go with me?"

"Why? Where are you going?"

"Not far, I want you to see something that I want to buy. The woman at the store called me earlier and said it was ready."

"Logan you're talking in riddles."

She laughed. "Just come with me after dinner. We won't be long."

***

Logan drove and Brooke sat in the passenger seat of the truck. "So where is this store?" Logan turned off of A1A heading back into Atlantic Beach. "I don't know of any store back here."

"We're going to her house. She took it home with her."

"What is it exactly?"

"A surprise for you."

"Um…ok?"

They drove further into the area full of beautiful two and three story beachfront homes. Logan pulled into the horseshoe driveway of a Tudor style, crème colored two story house with a three car garage. She parked behind the gray Mercedes.

"Who lives here? Haven't I seen this house before?"

Logan kept silent and walked through the unlocked front door.

"Jillian, are you in here?"

"Yes, I'm in the kitchen." A very attractive, slender woman in a skirt suit with jet black hair came around the corner as Logan and Brooke walked through the foyer. The beginning of the house had Oak colored hardwood floors and a staircase in the center that split off and swirled around going to two separate loft style rooms that took up the entire second floor.

"Logan, it's good to see you again." They shook hands. Brooke glanced around in awe of the gorgeous house. "This is my fiancé, Brooke McCabe, Brooke this is Jillian Cramer, my realtor." Brookes head swung around, she realized now that the house was empty. She shook the woman's hand.

"Is this place for sale? It's beautiful."

"As a matter of fact, I believe it's still on the market." She turned towards Logan.

"Really, Logan this place would be perfect for us." She continued walking around and noticed the place had five bedrooms, four bathrooms, a formal living room, a den, a kitchen with a bar and an island, a separate dining room and an in ground pool with an attached hot tub. Not to mention is was beachfront with private access. Both of the rooms upstairs had balconies. The kitchen had Italian tile floors and Marble counter tops. All of the rooms had carpeted floors. It reminded Brooke of Logan's high class Modern style Condo. She tried not to let herself fall for this house. "Although, it *is* rather large for only two people. I'm sure it's out of our price range anyway."

Logan smiled and pulled an envelope out of her back pocket.

"I believe you can take this house off of the market now, Jillian." Logan said as she handed her the envelope. Brooke's bottom jaw hit the floor. "It's all there, everything we spoke about."

"Great, you'll both need to be in my office on Monday to sign the final papers."

"What just happened?" Brooke turned towards Logan with a confused look on her face.

"I saw you looking at this house when we were driving around out here a few weeks ago. I called Jillian and had her meet me here to take a look at the inside, once I saw it; I knew you'd love it so I made an offer when those people made me an offer on the Condo."

"Oh my god Logan, you didn't discuss this with me first? How could you buy a house and not even let me see it? I don't work like that Logan." Brooke's voice was firm.

"Sweetheart, I emailed you pictures of the inside after I met with Jillian. It was furnished then because the owners were still living here. You told me how much you liked it so I had her start the papers. I wasn't going to do anything without you seeing the house first. I know this is a decision we are making together. I just didn't want to lose the house, plus I received the offer on the Condo and I needed to give them an answer."

Brooke was happy and mad at the same time. She knew she loved the house, but she was aggravated at Logan for not talking to her. "I understand why you did it. I just wish you would have discussed this with me first. This house is perfect and I'm happy that it's going to be ours."

"It *is* ours. I just gave Jillian the check from the bank."

"When do we have to be out of the Condo?"

"The movers are coming the week we are gone for the wedding."

"Movers?"

"Yeah, we need to have the valuable items boxed up already, but they box up everything else, as well as, taking apart all of the furniture and the TV and move all of it to the new house and unload it. We need to give them a schematic of how we want it set up, but they basically do it all, except of course, my office at the Condo, and our office here. We'll pack that stuff up and take care of it ourselves. They'll move the furniture for us though."

"That's good, I was wondering how we were going to do this by ourselves."

"The only thing we need to worry about is what we're wearing on September tenth, and the Celtic Pattern for our rings. The jeweler has called me three times this week." Logan shot Brooke a raised eyebrow.

"I love the one that you picked from your Scottish Heritage. He should be able to make them a continuous Celtic Knot, and add the four slightly raised diamonds across the top."

"Those will look really nice. I like that idea."

"Good, then it's settled, I'll call him in the morning."

"Well Ladies, if we seem to have everything straightened out here, I'll head back to my office and start drawing up the papers. Like I said, both of you need to be at my office Monday around nine a.m. to sign everything. Oh and Logan, you'll need to be there to sign over the Condo paperwork after you return from your honeymoon. Congratulations ladies!"

Logan shook the woman's hand. "Thank you so much Jillian, I'm glad you were able to make this all come together for us." *If the reality hasn't hit you yet Logan, it will now. You're getting married in six weeks, you sold your completely paid off million dollar Condo, and bought a two million dollar house. Holy Shit. Greer!*

***

The following week Logan invited Lynnie to meet her and Brooke for dinner and drinks at a restaurant close by.

"Hey, Babe." Lynnie gave Logan a hug. She turned to Brooke. "You must be Brooke, I've heard a lot about you, in a very short time." Lynnie smiled and shook her hand.

"It's nice to meet you, Lynnie." Brooke smiled back.

"Behave Lynnie, there's no need to tell her all of my bad habits in one night." Logan laughed.

"Oh come on...hmm where the hell do I start?"

"Lynnie!"

"Calm down, grouch. All I will say is congratulations to you both. And tell her how much of a good friend you are and how I've seen you through a lot, especially this last year."

"Yeah." Logan turned to Brooke. "We're good drinking buddies."

201

"Real good drinking buddies!" Lynnie chimed in.

"Is that so?" Brooke questioned.

"Hell yeah, should I tell her about Women's Fest?" Lynnie asked, knowing she had already let the cat out of the bag.

"Lynnie, no!" Logan's eyes grew large.

"What happened there? What is that?" Brooke looked confused.

"Sweetheart, it's a big festival for lesbians down in the Florida Keys. Remember me telling you about Lynnie's band?"

"Yeah."

"Well they were playing down there so I went down there and partied with them all weekend. Long story short..." Lynnie cut Logan off.

"Don't let her sweeten the story. She got wasted and passed out in a pool chair. I found her the next morning and pushed her ass in." Lynnie was laughing as she told the story.

"Oh my god, Logan." Brooke laughed.

"The best part is I drug her ass in with me."

"Yeah she did, chair and all." Everyone was laughing.

"No, the best part is me and Logan got out of the pool and went straight to the little café for breakfast soaking wet."

"No way, you guys are crazy." Brooke was still laughing. "Honey, I didn't know you had a wild side."

"You're kidding right?" Lynnie questioned Brooke.

"Uh Lynnie, let's stick to one story at time. Sweetie, me and Lynnie have had some good times over the years. Let's just leave it at that."

***

Lynnie and Brooke immediately hit it off, Logan was happy to see her best friend and fiancé getting along so well. The hard part was yet to come. Unfortunately, Chaney wasn't going to meet Brooke until after the wedding because their schedules were conflicting for the next couple of months.

Three weeks until the wedding, Logan and Brooke were asleep when Logan's cell phone rang, then Brooke's, as if in perfect harmony. *Oh no!* Logan scampered in the dark to the flashing light and ringing tone.

"Agent Greer."

"Logan, this is Walter Hudson, a plane crash landed into Chicago's O'Hare Airport. You'll need to be there ASAP."

She took a deep breath. "How bad is it?"

"I don't have full details, all I know is it crashed into another plane as it was coming down the runway. I'll email you everything as soon as I get it. You need to get in the air now. You're flight leaves in an hour."

"Yes Sir." She hung up and looked over at Brooke who had also just closed her phone.

"O'Hare?" They said simultaneously.

***

They flew out together. Logan led the detail team once everyone arrived. She gathered all of them together before they went out to the runway.

"Listen up, I'm Agent Greer with the NTSB, I

have Brooke McCabe here with me from the FAA. It appears as if we have a DC9 that collided with a 727 at the end of the Tarmac. From my reports there are no casualties on either plane, thankfully. But, there is an extensive amount of damage and injuries. We'll need half of you to get statements from all of the passengers and crew. The other half of you need to locate the black boxes and get them up and running. With a little bit of luck and a hell of a lot of hard work we can be out of here in two weeks. Are there any questions?"

When no one raised a hand, Logan hustled everyone into the airport security trucks and led them out to the planes. The DC9's nose was smashed in. The 727's nose was also smashed. The pilot and co-pilot on both planes were seriously injured. Logan walked around both planes examining the wrecked areas. Her crew began working feverously. By the end of the day she had all of the statements and was waiting for the CVR and FDR to upload into the computer from the black boxes.

"Don't get yourself all stressed out sweetie, we can postpone the wedding if we need to." Logan turned towards the beautiful, innocent voice.

"I love you so much, and we *are* getting married in three weeks, come hell or high water."

Brooke smiled. "I love you too."

***

Logan sat in the airport hangar with the two damaged airplanes and the rest of the investigation crew. She grabbed her cell phone and hit speed dial number one.

"Walter Hudson."

"Hey, this is Agent Greer."

"Hey, how are we coming in Chicago?"

"Not bad, this was a simple incident, caused by the ATC. The DC9 was sitting on Lane A waiting to take off and the 727 had just landed and was instructed to take Lane A back to the terminal. When the 727 turned the corner it ran slap into the DC9 that was instructed to move out onto the runway for take off. It's not too big of a mess, so it'll take another week to finish the reports and then we should be out of here."

"Sounds good."

A week later they were wrapping up the investigation. Airport miscommunication between the ATC and the pilots caused the accident. Logan was at her make-shift desk typing her reports when her cell rang.

"Agent Greer."

"I hear you're playing with crashed airplanes in Chicago."

"Hey Chaney, how'd you know?"

"I'm in town for a Comedy show. I saw the news and figured you were here."

"We should get together for dinner, Brooke's here with me working too."

"Sounds good."

***

Logan was on pins and needles when she and Brooke walked into the restaurant. She hoped her ex-wife approved of her future wife. *How awkward does that sound?* She thought.

"Hey you!" Chaney stood and gave Logan a hug. Brooke smiled and shook her hand. She was impressed.

The woman in front of her was even more beautiful than the pictures in Logan's office at the Condo.

"It's nice to meet you, I've heard a lot about you." Chaney spoke first.

"Likewise, I have to say I'm a fan, I like your show." Brooke hoped her nervousness didn't show.

"Thank you." Chaney knew what Logan saw in this woman, she was as charming as she was beautiful. She thought she looked like an angel with tan skin and long honey colored hair. Her smile could melt the strongest of hearts.

Everyone ordered dinner and Chaney took it upon herself to order a nice bottle of wine for the table.

"So, how's the government going to handle you guys being married and working for different agencies?" Chaney questioned as she sipped her wine.

"So far we haven't had any problems. I seriously doubt we will anyway. They would be stupid to try something."

"Yeah, but you know how right-wing our government is."

"It would be one hell of a lawsuit if they did try to fire us or cause problems." Brooke chimed in.

Chaney raised her glass. "Here's to the two of you being happy together." All of their glasses clinked together.

"Thank you." Brooke smiled.

***

After dinner they left the restaurant together. Chaney smiled at Logan and told her how happy she was for her. Logan walked over to the valet booth to turn in both tickets and Chaney leaned close to Brooke.

"She loves you a lot and I can tell you love her. I don't want to see her hurt. I care for her a lot and will always love her. I really am happy for the both of you."

Brooke smiled. "Thank you."

"I know everything that has happened between you two. I was the one that helped pick her back up after you ran her over."

Brooke took a deep breath, not sure what to say.

Chaney continued to speak. "Take care of her and treat her right. She will do everything in her power to give you the world." She smiled.

Logan returned and Chaney pulled two tickets out of her pocket. "Here, come see my show tonight."

"Oh cool, I'd love to see you on stage." Brooke was excited.

"I'll go on one condition." Logan said seriously.

"What's that?"

"You don't mention me."

"Do I ever?" Chaney questioned.

***

With the hardest part behind her, Logan felt a giant weight lifted off of her shoulders. *Next week should be a piece of cake.* Logan and Brooke walked into the theatre.

"She's a really nice person. I enjoyed dinner." Brooke turned to Logan.

"Yeah, I don't know what I'd do without her sometimes."

"Do you miss being married to her?"

"No, I miss being close to her. We have always

207

been best friends. We grew apart as lovers. That was both of our faults. But, I'm happy with my life and happy that she is still in it. Besides, I love you and cannot wait to be married to you."

"That's good because I can't wait either." She smiled from ear to ear and squeezed Logan's hand.

***

Chaney walked out on stage to begin her show.

"Good evening ladies and gentlemen. I'd like to make a small announcement real quick." The audience was quiet as Chaney continued. "I may be a little more nervous than usual tonight, you see, my ex-wife is in the room." The crowd applauded. "Yes but you see she's not alone." They audience laughed. "She's with her soon-to-be *new* wife!" Everyone in the crowd was laughing hysterically. "But it's okay." Chaney hesitated. "I just met her for the first time an hour ago at dinner." Everyone laughed again. "On a serious note, I want to say congratulations to you both." Chaney went back to her comedy monologue.

Fourteen

Logan and Brooke were 'lei'd' in Honolulu tradition as they stepped off the plane. Brooke grabbed Logan's hand and squeezed. Logan turned towards her and smiled. "Welcome to paradise."

"Hold that thought until the end of the Honeymoon because if this phone goes off I'm going to run it over with an airplane."

"Don't worry about it sweetheart. We're here now and I don't plan on leaving until you're my wife."

"Good, I don't plan on leaving here either, at least not until my last name is Greer." Brooke said with a smile.

"Really?"

"Yes, I wanted to surprise you, I had the papers drawn up while we were in Chicago. I signed everything yesterday so as soon as we're married my last name changes."

"Wow, that's really special. I figured you were going to keep your name." Logan pulled Brooke against her and kissed her lips. She desperately tried to contain herself and not ravish Brooke's body in the middle of the airport. "I love you so much."

"I love you too."

***

Twenty-four hours until the wedding, Brooke was checking the last minute preparations, most importantly the weather. She and Logan went down to the bar to have a few drinks to celebrate their last single night together.

"Are you ready for this?"

"Yeah, you?"

"I was born ready!" Logan shouted as they downed the triple Patron shots with a splash of lime. Brooke winced at the tangy burning sensation in her throat and chest. Logan smiled with ease and had the bartender set up another round.

"Who got you drinking this shit?"

"Lynnie. Who else?"

"I don't wanna be sick tomorrow. You do the next set."

"Huh uh, not alone." Logan shook her head as she spoke. "Last one sweetie."

They tipped the glasses together once more. "Okay, I've had enough of that shit." She ordered a Guinness and Logan ordered a Foster's. They finished their beers and took a walk along the beach, stopping at the exact spot where the ceremony was suppose to take place.

"Sundown tomorrow I'll be standing right here next to the most beautiful woman I have ever laid eyes on, as she becomes my wife."

Brooke squeezed Logan's hand. "I'm the lucky one."

"Nah…okay…well maybe…no, I'd say I was luckier."

"How so?"

Fate Vs. Destiny

Logan swept Brooke up into her arms, and carried her closer to the water and laid her in the sand. Their lips met softly at first, burning together as their tongues tasted the remnants of the alcohol. Brooke's hands were tangled in Logan's hair. Logan had one arm around Brooke and the other hand slid under her shirt to fondle taut nipples. She ran her palm against the soft skin, down to the low cut waistline of Brooke's pants. Her hand went under the band easily and discovered Brooke wasn't wearing panties when she found the silky patch of hair. She smiled and continued teasingly kissing the magnificent woman under her. Brooke arched her back as two of Logan's fingers ran across the throbbing muscles around her clit and then deep inside of her.

"Ah…" She gasped and ran her short nails along Logan's back with every thrust she pulled Logan tighter and tighter against her until it was over. She looked up into moonlit iridescent green eyes and rolled Logan onto her back. "My turn…"

"Is that so…" Brooke was past the layers of clothing and deep inside Logan before she could finish her seductive sentence. Logan was breathing ragged breaths separated by faint gasps as Brooke went deeper then pulled her fingers out to tease her clit with slow circles before going back in.

Minutes later both women were laying in each other arms in the moonlight, covered in sand, and listening to the waves crash against the shore a few feet away.

***

They spent the next day making sure everything

211

was set for their ceremony and stopped for a late lunch before going back to the hotel.

"I can't believe that in a few hours we will be married." Logan looked at Brooke quizzically.

"Is that a bad thing? Are you having second thoughts?"

"No sweetie, I'm excited." Brooke rushed over to Logan and threw her arms around her neck. "I love you so much!"

Logan kissed her, letting her lips linger softly. "I love you too!"

Just before sundown on the North Shore Logan dressed in a thin, short, white halter top dress with no shoes and Brooke dressed in a thin, short, white spaghetti strap dress with no shoes. They walked hand in hand down the beach through the area lit up by tiki torches and two rows of white roses as the music played. They had chosen to walk down the isle together since they wanted a private ceremony and didn't invite their families to join them. A woman in white cloth stood at the end of the isle. Not overly religious, but holy enough for both of them to exchange vows.

As the sun set behind the ocean, Brooke and Logan were pronounced a married couple. They cried together as they donned sparkling rings on their left hands, and ear to ear smiles. They walked back through the flowers and tiki torches up to the hotel restaurant's open deck where champagne and wedding cake were served along with music and dancing for the hotel guests that came down to celebrate with them. They already planned an enormous party for their friends and family at home once they were back and settled into their new life together.

***

As Aerosmith's song 'Crazy' played they danced together. Logan smiled. "So, how does it feel to be Mrs. Greer?"

Brooke still had tears in her eyes as she smiled back. "I've never been this happy in my entire life Logan."

"Good because I can't imagine life without you. I love you so much sweetheart."

"I love you too." Brooke kissed Logan passionately. "I can't wait to get you up to that room." She whispered seductively.

About the Author

Graysen Morgen was born and raised in North Florida with winding rivers and waterways at her back door and the white sandy beach a mile away. She has spent most of her lifetime in the sun and on the water. She enjoys reading, writing, fishing, and spending as much time as possible with her partner and their daughter.

You can contact Graysen at graysenmorgen@aol.com and like her fan page on facebook.com/graysenmorgen

Made in the USA
Las Vegas, NV
08 April 2022